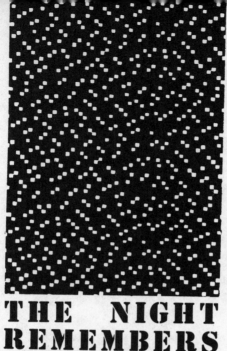

THE NIGHT REMEMBERS

THE NIGHT
REMEMBERS

Ed Gorman

St. Martin's Press New York

Design by Diane Stevenson/SNAP•HAUS GRAPHICS

Library of Congress Cataloging-in-Publication Data

Gorman, Edward.
      The night remembers : a Jack Walsh mystery / Ed Gorman.
        p. cm.
      ISBN 0-312-05482-3
      I. Title.
   PS3557.0759N54 1991   813'.54—dc20   90-15550

10 9 8 7 6 5 4 3 2

This is for Bill Pronzini and somebody else who shall re-main Nameless.

This manuscript went through several drafts. My associate Barb Kramer was with me through every one. Thanks, Barb.

Thanks also to Ruth Ashby for her considerable contributions to this book.

I would also like to thank Sheriff Dennis Blome for his help with this novel.

—E.G.

"The Child"

Without meaning to they stand watching
while it plays; occasionally the round
living face emerges from the profile,
clear and whole like some ripened hour

that rises and chimes unto its end.
But the others don't keep track of the strokes,
dim from toil and sluggish from life;
and they don't even notice how it bears—,

how it bears everything, even then, still,
when wearily in its small clothes dressed up
beside them as if in the waiting room
it sits and keeps on waiting for its time.

—Rainer Maria Rilke

THE NIGHT REMEMBERS

1

"Hello."

"Is Faith there?" I said.

"Not right now. I'm Marcia."

"Marcia?"

"The babysitter. I live in the building. I work the night shift at Rockwell. On the line. That's why I can babysit this morning."

"Oh. Where's Faith?"

"I'm not sure."

"She didn't say?"

"Not exactly."

"Marcia."

"Yes."

"I'd like to ask you a question."

"All right."

"Is there something you're not telling me?"

"Is this Mr. Walsh?"

"Yes. Why?"

"She said you'd probably be calling."

"Oh. Did she say anything else?"

Hesitation. "Just that I wasn't, uh, supposed to say anything."

"Say anything about what?"

Hesitation. "Well, you know, the way she left and all."

"What about the way she left?"

Hesitation. "She'll get mad. You know her temper."

"I know her temper."

"So maybe I shouldn't say anything."

"I'm right across the street, Marcia. I can walk over there easily enough."

Sigh. "God, you make it sound like a threat or something."

That, anyway, had been my intention. "So what about how she left?"

"Well."

"Marcia, we're wasting time."

"Well, she was crying."

"Do you know about what?"

Hesitation. "I'm not sure."

"Sure you're sure. Now tell me."

"Well, she found something."

"Found something?"

Hesitation. "It probably isn't anything. I mean, I've got a cousin named Rosie and she found the same thing and the doctor told her it wasn't anything to worry about at all. She has to go back and get it checked every six months or so, but she's fine. Just fine."

"What did she find?"

"I really don't think I should say any more, Mr. Walsh."

"Did Faith tell you how much I care about her?"

"Huh-uh."

"Well, I care about her a lot."

"She said you're a nice man."

"Well, Marcia, put yourself in my place."

"Huh?"

"You call up and a stranger answers and she says she's babysitting and that Faith is gone."

"Oh. Right."

"And furthermore, she tells you that Faith has 'found something' and then she mentions something about a doctor and a cousin named Rosie who has to go back every six months for a checkup. Do you think that would scare you, Marcia?"

"I guess, sure."

"Then you'll tell me?"

"It's just a lump. I really don't think it's a big deal at all."

"A lump?"

"Yeah. On one of her breasts. That's what she found this morning. You know how she gets. Sort of hysterical. I'm not putting her down or anything, but she does kind of overreact sometimes."

"I suppose she does, yes. So where did she go?"

"To her doctor's office. She took a cab."

"Oh."

"So I'm watching Hoyt."

Hoyt is a year-and-a-half. His favorite food is from Dairy Queen. His favorite TV show is "Sesame Street." Faith insists I am Hoyt's father. I am not convinced of that as yet. "Did she say when she'd be back?"

"Probably two hours or so."

"And she left when?"

"About an hour ago."

"I'd like you to do me a favor."

"Sure."

"I'd like you to leave her a note that says to call me as soon as possible. I'll be at my office."

"All right, Mr. Walsh. I'll write it out right now before I forget it."

I said thank you and hung up.

2

That was how Wednesday morning began. With Faith Hallahan, a thirty-two-year-old woman thirty-two years my junior, finding a lump on her breast and rushing off to the doctor's.

After talking with Marcia I went out to the parking lot of the apartment house I manage and got into my blue 1978 Pontiac Firebird. I was stunned enough by the news about Faith that I just sat behind the wheel for a time. I had a cigarette, one of the six a day I was allowing myself of late, and I watched Mr. Fredericks, an aged black man who always seemed to be wearing the same gray cardigan, the same denim work shirt buttoned tight at the top, and the same gray wrinkled work pants. He used to be a postman. He retired when he was fifty-seven and lived for two years in Florida until he found out his Miami daughter was a prostitute. An angry man and a religious man, he found himself incapable of forgiving her and moved back here to Cedar Rapids. He told me all this one Christmas Eve when neither of us had anything better to do than become friends of a vague but necessary sort. Now, he pulled the lid off a garbage can and slammed a greasy grocery sack inside the can with exceptionally violent grace. After putting the lid back, he became aware of my gaze, looked up, and stared at me. He shook his head as if he'd caught me doing something despicable and then went back inside the three-story brick apartment house called The Alma.

Rather than have another tenant get suspicious about me sitting out in my car (What would they think? Suicide? Masturbation? Some sort of stroke?), I worked the gas pedal carefully—you couldn't give her too much or too little—and left the parking lot.

"You look surprised to see me," Irma said.

"Not at all."

"I shouldn't be here?"

"Of course you should be here."

"I realize I'm not a licensed private investigator, but I've picked up a few things over the years."

"I'm sure you have."

"You want some coffee?"

"God, that would be great."

"Then why don't you go get us some down at the Big Boy? I'd like cream in mine if you don't mind."

"My pleasure," I said, and left.

Ozmanski and I were members of the Linn County Sheriff's Office a total of sixty-one years—thirty for me and thirty-one for him. Both detectives. We'd met over in Salerno during World War II, just as things were turning the right way for the Yanks. We bowled, fished, drank, played shuffleboard, and, after retirement, opened up a small investigative agency in downtown Cedar Rapids, in one of those gray four-story stone buildings that are falling, one by one, to urban renewal. Mostly our shop does two types of work—trial backgrounds for defense attorneys and background checks for employers. We were in business two years before Ozmanski ran his new Dodge Dart into the rear end of a bread truck out on 149. And died. Everybody assumed he was drinking. Being his partner, I had to defend him and say hey bullshit you knew

Don better than that. But I assumed he was drinking, too.

Three weeks ago, four months after Don's death, his widow, Irma, started showing up. Not every day. Just once in a while. "To pick up," she'd say. So she'd dust or sweep or ask me if I had any typing that needed doing. The hell of it was, Irma and I had never much gotten along. My dead wife, Sharon, always called Irma a gossip and a troublemaker, and she'd been absolutely right. Every time Sharon and I had any sort of spat, Irma would start the story, under the guise of great sorrow, that we were on the verge of a divorce. She didn't single us out. She spread such stories about everybody. So now when I was nice to her I felt I was being disloyal to Sharon. That probably didn't make a hell of a lot of sense, but when you think about it, very little does.

I got two big paper containers of coffee and walked back to the office. The temperature was fifty-seven and downtown Cedar Rapids was beautiful in the Indian summer day, morning sunlight golden off the windows of the brokerage houses, the breeze soft and warm off the Cedar River two blocks away. At my age, though, you keep flashing back to the way things used to be. I could still taste the strawberry malts Woolworth used to serve at their lunch counter, and the tang of the pickles on their cheeseburgers. Up the street from Woolworth had been the Palace Theater, a second-run place just right for a cop and his family. They'd played a lot of James Cagney and Humphrey Bogart movies for Sharon and me and a lot of Francis the Talking Mule films for the kids. There is absolutely no evidence of Woolworth's or the theater's existence now. They might have belonged to a lost race. Today the downtown is largely a business and financial center unexpected and impressive in a small city like this one, with BMWs and Mercedes-Benzes wheeling around the streets. I still miss the Palace and eating at Tony's next door with my family and listening to Jo Stafford and Nat "King" Cole on the jukebox.

* * *

"Visitor."

"Huh?"

"You got a visitor."

"Oh."

"You won't believe who she is."

I sat her coffee down on the desk and leaned forward to her. Irma is twenty-five pounds overweight, always wears a little-girl blue ribbon in her iron-gray hair (sort of like Petunia Pig, actually), and tends to flowered housedresses that she obviously feels hide her bulk. "Sound carries in this place." I put a finger to my lips. "If I've got a visitor in there, then she probably heard every word you said."

"Oh. I'm sorry."

"No problem, Irma. You just have to whisper is all."

She splayed her hands. "So I'll whisper from now on." She sounded defensive and maybe even irritated.

"Good."

The outer office where Irma sat doubles as the reception area and the working office. You can't work for long in the other office. Too hot. In the winter the steam heat gets over-whelming. In the summer direct sunlight broils the place. About all you can do is have brief conferences with clients and then get out of there. That's why you'll find the reception area packed with two desks, two upright manual typewriters, two phones, and three filing cabinets. And a lot of dust. In a building this old—in stone just above our window is a piece of fancy carving that reads In God We Trust 1888—dust set-tles slowly but without mercy. It's a perpetual process and God help you if you've got bad sinuses.

"You got any typing or anything?" Irma said. Now she sounded hurt.

"Irma, it's great having you here. I'm sorry I kind of snapped at you."

"It really is? Great having me here?"

Why had I lied? It was terrible having her here. Maybe if I'd kept up the mean stuff she'd have taken the hint and done what she was always threatening to do, go live with her oldest boy up near Green Bay, Wisconsin, the professor who was always in trouble because he was the only supporter of Lyndon LaRouche on the entire faculty. (I'd always voted Democratic, even for McGovern though that had been a pretty tough lever to pull, and that had always bugged the hell out of Ozmanski.)

"This coffee is delightful," Irma said. "You got just the right amount of cream."

I heard all the loneliness and grieving in her voice then and felt, as I usually do, like a total slug. I remembered the way she'd sobbed in spasms at graveside when they'd lowered Don into the ground in his coffin, the sound of that first thrumming shovel of dirt throwing her back in her seat as if she'd been shot. A total slug I was.

I raised my paper cup and saluted her. "Nice to have you here."

Then I went into the other office.

She sat in a perfect blue suit in perfect blue pumps with a perfect blue leather bag on her lap. She had once been beautiful, but even with a few laugh lines at mouth and eyes, even with a little loose flesh on the neck, she was still damn near perfect, one of those prim, trim women who never quite lose their appeal no matter how old they get. Her, I put at forty-five to fifty.

As I closed the door behind me, I noticed how the sunlight made a nimbus of her frosted hair. "Hello," I said.

"You don't remember me, do you?"

I walked into the room. It contained a couch and two wing chairs the building manager had found in the basement. His guess was that they'd belonged to two women who'd run an interior decorating service. Over in the corner was a dead 19″ Motorola black and white TV set. It hadn't worked since the

Cubs had started using lights at the ballpark. Maybe the set was protesting.

I looked at her more carefully, which was certainly a pleasure, but still I saw nothing familiar about her.

Then I remembered what Irma had said: "You won't believe who she is."

I sat down in the facing wing chair. "I'm sorry if I sound rude."

"Then you don't remember?"

"I'm afraid I don't."

"Pennyfeather. George Pennyfeather."

Then I remembered. Of course. "And you're—"

"Mrs. Pennyfeather. Lisa."

"That's right."

"How is—" I stopped myself. I'd been about to ask, How is he doing these days? But that probably isn't the right kind of casual social question to ask about somebody you helped put in prison.

"He's out. Just last week."

"I'm happy for you."

"It's been a long twelve years."

"I'm sure it has." I realized now why Irma had been so amused at the presence of this woman in our office. Most ex-convicts don't send their wives to see the detective who conducted the investigation that ultimately landed them in the slammer.

"He's still innocent, Mr. Walsh. He was when you put him in prison, and he is to this day."

"I see."

"I'm embarrassing you, aren't I?"

"A little, I suppose."

"I don't mean to. I'm speaking without recrimination. I'm simply stating the facts."

"Oh."

"We don't even blame you for thinking he was guilty."

"He was guilty, Mrs. Pennyfeather. He really was."

She waved a sweet little hand dismissively. She even had a perfectly sad little smile for me. "I know you hear this all the time. How this man or that was framed. Over the past twelve years I've gotten to know a number of women whose husbands are in prison. Almost all of them believe their husbands are innocent."

"That's a natural defense mechanism. It's how you deal with that particular kind of grief is all."

"You're awfully philosophical for a policeman."

"Ex-policeman. And not all of us move our lips when we read."

"I've embarrassed you again."

"I'm just not really fond of stereotypes."

Something I said seemed to amuse her. "How about the stereotype of the meek little accountant who couldn't deal with his wife's infidelity in any other way but to kill her lover? That's been a cliché ever since I was a girl, anyway." She opened her blue leather bag, which even from here looked expensive, and took out something that almost shocked me: a package of Lucky Strikes. Women of her generation still smoked—despite all the Surgeon General's reports and rough TV advertising to the contrary—but probably not many of them smoked Luckies. She tamped a cigarette against the pack and then put it between red lips that parted perfectly to receive it. She clicked on a tiny gold lighter and got her cigarette going and then threw her head back and let a long blue stream of smoke escape her mouth. With a delicate fingertip, she daubed a minuscule fleck of tobbaco from one of her gorgeous lips.

"First of all, he was never my lover."

"Karl Jankov, you mean?"

"Yes. Karl Jankov. That's not to say that I didn't consider it. At the time, George was having a few—problems, and my life was fairly miserable." She blew out some more smoke and then looked at me with a gaze that managed to be both harsh and seductive. "George and I came from very different backgrounds."

"Your father was a prominent state senator, correct?"

"Yes. He even served a term in Washington, but he was thrown out during the Goldwater debacle. I've always resented that. My father was a very moderate Republican. It's terrible how people blame you for things you didn't do." She stopped herself. A tint of red was in her cheeks. "I wasn't making a reference to George."

"I know."

"I suppose I've grown into this victim attitude. All the years waiting for him to be set free."

"I'd like to ask you a question."

"I'm sure I know what it is." She sighed. Her small hands fidgeted on the surface of her purse. "Why did I come here to see you?"

I nodded.

She put her head down. I looked over at the Merchants Bank building. It filled most of the westerly window.

She raised her head. There was an angry dignity in her eyes now. I would pay for trifling with her, her gaze said.

"I want to hire you."

"I see."

"You hide your shock well."

"Years of practice."

"It makes sense when you think about it."

"What makes sense?"

"My hiring you to prove that George is innocent."

"What?"

"That time it showed. Your nostrils flared a little bit and your eyes narrowed. But why else would I be hiring you, Mr. Walsh?"

"I'm the man who arrested him."

"Believe me, I'm quite aware of that. As is my entire family.

At Christmastime Carolyn, my youngest child, used to work herself into a frenzy thinking about her father sitting in prison and you home enjoying yourself. Oh, believe me, Mr. Walsh, I'm quite well aware of what you've done."

"And you still want to hire me?"

"Who knows the case better?"

"It's been a long time."

"But you'll have access to all the records. Spend an afternoon with them and you'll be caught up to date in no time. I've hired several detectives over the years, and they got nowhere."

I said, "I'm not sure I'll be taking any cases anyway. Not for the foreseeable future."

"Oh? Is something wrong?" She leaned forward in the wing chair like an animal that had suddenly sensed something amiss.

"A friend of mine may be ill. I just can't make any commitments." I tried to picture Faith in the doctor's waiting room. She'd be biting her fingernails and solemnly shaking her head, convinced that the worst possible fate awaited her.

"That is it, then."

"What is?"

"Your slight air of being distracted."

"You're observant."

"I haven't had much else to be the past twelve years. There were friends who thought I should get divorced and friends who thought I should run away and friends who thought I should date. I did none of those things. I sat in our very large house and looked out our very large window and sometimes it would snow and sometimes it would rain and sometimes the sun would be shining and then one day I looked at my son, David, and he was a twenty-five-year-old graduating law school and getting married. And Carolyn was in college. And I was alone. That's when I became observant, Mr. Walsh. Loneliness does that to you—it's a survival technique, I think.

You become very aware of deceit and dishonesty on the part of those around you."

"I'm sorry for the life you've had."

"So you don't see any chance that you were wrong?"

"There's always that possibility."

"How diplomatic."

"But I don't think I was. Not as I remember things, anyway."

"If I wasn't Karl's lover, then George would have had no reason to kill him."

"Actually consummating the relationship is irrelevant. People get threatened over things as small as glances and smiles. If your husband was having 'problems,' as you describe them, he was probably predisposed to anger anyway."

She looked at me not with dislike but a certain pity. "How easy life must be for you, Mr. Walsh."

"It's not easy at all."

"To be so certain of yourself and all your perceptions. So certain."

"I think you can see why it's probably not a good idea I work for you."

She stood up. She exhaled the last of her Lucky, blue smoke against the golden stream of sunlight. She put out a slight hand and I shook it. For the first time I saw some sign of what this visit must have cost her. Her mouth had begun to quiver, and her eyes were wet with tears.

"I'm sorry for my sake that you're not more open-minded, Mr. Walsh," she said.

I started to open the door for her, but she stopped me with an upraised hand. She opened the door for herself and went out. She shut the door very quietly. If she'd slammed it, I could have just dismissed her as another crank. But the quiet way reminded me of her lovely sad eyes and the disappointment I had put in them. I would remember those eyes far longer than I would a slamming door.

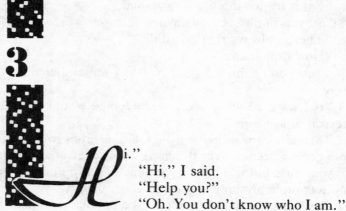

3

"Hi."

"Hi," I said.

"Help you?"

"Oh. You don't know who I am."

"Gee, no, I don't."

"I'm Walsh."

"Oh, Mr. *Walsh*. C'mon in."

"I can hear Hoyt."

"Yeah. He's got some kind of rash. Nothing serious but—Why're we standing out here? C'mon in. I'm Marcia Ramey, by the way. The babysitter you talked to on the phone."

"Right."

"Anyways, I'm Marcia and she isn't back yet."

"Oh."

"Shouldn't be long though."

The apartment was, as always, impeccable, filled with rattan furnishings and hanging plants and huge abstract paintings done in earth tones and signifying nothing. The modular couch was white, as was the daybed pushed against the wall. The floors had been stripped to bare beautiful wood and polished with painstaking and neurotic love. It was one of the few places I'd ever been that looked *better* than magazine layouts.

"You like some coffee?"

"No thanks, Marcia."

"You want me to get Hoyt?"

"If you wouldn't mind."

"Like I said, he's kind of crabby."

She went and got Hoyt. He wore clean blue pajamas with feet in them. He smelled wonderfully of baby oil and baby powder. She put him on my knee.

"Don't let him sit too square on his bottom," she said. "That's where the rash is."

"Uh-huh."

So we played, Hoyt and I, and I forgot all about Marcia Ramey. I goo-gooed with him, I tickled his chin, I combed his soft blond hair with my fingers, I made silly faces that he took in with his somber blue eyes, and I gave him my comb and let him comb my hair, something he never tires of doing. Hoyt is one of those infants you just know is going to be a linebacker somebody. If you saw him eat, you'd know why.

"He went number two."

"Huh?" I said.

"Number two. The poop shoot. He went."

"Hoyt did?"

"Sure, Hoyt. Who else?"

"I guess that's a good question."

"Anyway, he made lump-lump."

"How can you tell from across the room? I can't tell and he's sitting in my lap."

"I'm the oldest of six brothers and sisters. Mom had arthritis so I took care of all of them. You just develop a nose for that kind of thing, no pun intended."

For the first time, I really looked at Marcia Ramey. She gave the impression of being capable, even athletic, big but in no way fat, attractive if not quite pretty, and filled with the kind of durable good spirits that make you envious. She wore a man's work shirt and blue jeans and white socks and white Reeboks. She came over and snatched up Hoyt and took him into the bedroom and did what she had to. About halfway through the procedure, she got him laughing, something I hadn't been able to do.

I decided on the coffee. I was just raising the cup when I heard the key in the doorway.

She came in and said, "Oh. You're here."

I knew this wasn't the time for a joke. I just nodded.

She came in even farther and went over to the couch and sat herself down with a great deal of decorum. Ordinarily, she sort of flings herself onto it.

"How'd it go?"

"Not sure yet."

"Oh."

"Wish I was."

"I'll bet."

"I'd just as soon not talk about it while Marcia's here."

"I understand."

"Oh, Walsh, the hell with you. You never act like this and you know it."

"Like what?"

"Kissing my ass and being so polite."

"Tell me what you want me to do and I'll do it."

"Get lost. That's what I'd like you to do."

She sat there then and really started crying. Her whole body shook.

I went up to the bedroom door and said to Marcia, "You think it'd be all right if I closed this?"

"Faith come in?"

"Right."

We just sort of stared at each other.

She pantomimed, "Is she all right?" and kept pointing to her mouth as she did so, as if she needed to direct my eyesight as well as my hearing.

I grimaced and shook my head. I closed the door and went back and sat across from Faith.

Today she wore, from the feet up, penny loafers and argyle socks and designer jeans and a mint-green sweater that brought out the green of her eyes. She's red-haired with freckles. But don't think of the pug-nosed variety. No, hers is classical beauty—regal, imposing, and, even at times such as these, just a little arrogant. The hell of it is—for her sake anyway—she'd had one of those terrible childhoods that robbed her of any self-confidence her looks might have given her. "I'm only beautiful on the outside," she's fond of saying in her dramatic way.

"I'd like you to tell me what the doctor said."

"He didn't say anything."

"He didn't examine you?"

She kept right on crying. "Yes, he examined me."

"He didn't draw some conclusion?"

"Yes, he drew a conclusion."

"Well, that's the part I'm interested in. The conclusion part."

"He said he wasn't sure."

"Sure about what?"

"Wasn't sure if it was cancer or not."

"Oh."

So there you had it. The most dreaded word in our vocabulary. Sitting there in this really fine room with rattan and plants and fancy if incomprehensible paintings—and sitting there with a hauntingly good-looking woman—and then the whole thing got spoiled with one little word.

I started trembling. I wanted to cry. If Marcia hadn't been in the other room, I probably would have.

"I'm sure it's going to be all right."

"Please don't say stuff like that."

"I'm sorry."

"Do you know how infuriating shit like that is?"

"I know and I'm sorry and I won't say anything like it."

"Why don't you just slap me? I'm being such a bitch."

"You're perfectly fine."

"Any other time I was acting like this, you'd at least *think* of slapping me."

I decided to be honest. "Kiddo," I said, "this isn't any other time."

I went over and sat down beside her. I took her hand. It was very cold. I had a terrible image that it would feel like this when she died. I hated myself for thinking it.

"Why don't I fix you some lunch?"

"I'm not hungry."

"I'll bet you didn't have breakfast."

"No, I didn't."

"Then at least let me fix you some soup. You don't even have to drink it. You can just sip it. Like tea or coffee."

"You're a pretty decent guy, Walsh, you know that? Even if you won't admit Hoyt's your son."

"You still got all that tomato soup I bought you on sale that time?"

For the first time, she smiled, sniffling as she did so. "You bought me so much of that crap, Walsh, there'll be soup up there after I'm dead."

Then she realized what she'd said and started crying again.

4

Ordinarily, young Master Banister comes on Saturday morning, which is when the BMWs and the Porsches and the Volvos invade our neighborhood. These are the lawyers and CPAs and doctors who own the apartment buildings that have bloomed in the wake of the old Victorian houses that once made Third Avenue so spectacular on sunny Sunday drives. "Rental property" is the correct term. Fill up the apartments and you not only get your bank payment made for you, you also make enough net income to invest in other rental property. Pretty soon you can afford to *hire* somebody like me as your live-in manager.

Anyway, young Master Banister arrived late that Wednesday afternoon, just as the skies turned black and a chill rain began to fall. He and his wife were, he said, headed for Chicago, some sort of Northwestern class reunion, and he needed to check things out with me now since he wouldn't be here Saturday. He hoped, he said, I didn't mind that he'd forgotten to call me in advance.

He brought, as usual, his checklist in the form of a single page of a small leatherbound notebook that he flipped through after carefully wetting the tip of one finger. He was approximately thirty-five with a short earnest haircut, black earnest horn-rim eyeglasses, an earnest white button-down shirt, an earnest blue five-button cardigan sweater, and a pair of earnest chinos that complemented his very earnest black and white saddle shoes. It was the wrong sissy touch, those shoes on a man his age, and it told me more than I wanted to know about young Master Banister.

"Why don't I run it down apartment by apartment?"

"Fine," I said.

"Mrs. Knapp in A?"

"Still complaining that her faucet leaks and keeps her awake."

"We checked it. It doesn't leak any more than all the others."

"All right."

"Mrs. Hester in B?"

"Nothing going on there."

"She still has the cat?"

"Yes."

"She get it declawed yet?"

"Yes."

"Good."

"I told her otherwise you'd evict her."

"You really want to make me the bad guy here, don't you? Is it my fault she's legally blind?"

"She just didn't want to hurt the cat. She said it would be like somebody ripping off her fingernails."

"Hardly."

"You want to ask me about C?"

"Is Mr. Wylie still playing that country western music so loud?"

"Yes, but Mrs. Gamble says she doesn't mind any more. She said she's gotten used to it."

"Fine. D?"

"I still don't think she's a hooker."

"You ever take a close look at her?"

"Of course I have. She's an attractive young woman."

"I still say she's a hooker. When Cindy and I pulled in here a few weeks ago, I saw a man walking her out to the sidewalk and he gave her money."

"Maybe it was her boyfriend."

"Does she have a boyfriend?"

"Not that I know of. But then I don't know everything."

"Implying I do, Mr. Walsh?"

"You want to know about E?"

"Is this the woman who made that remark about me?"

"Yes. Mrs. Kramer."

"She had no right to say what she did."

"You broke in while she was on the toilet."

"I hardly 'broke in.' I own this place. Plus, I didn't know anybody was there."

"Well, she hasn't made any other remarks about you."

"These people have just got to learn some respect." The way he said "these people," you knew he was talking about more than just the residents of The Alma. He meant all people who didn't drive BMWs and who didn't wear earnest black horn-rims and sissy saddle shoes.

"F?"

"F allegedly had the cockroaches?"

"Not allegedly. I saw them too."

"Winter should be here soon enough."

"And?"

"And winter usually takes care of cockroaches."

"Not these cockroaches."

He sighed. He wrote something in his little notebook. "I'll have the Orkin man come out here and have a look. How about G?"

"No problems there. Mrs. Fetzer is very happy now that you put in a new window."

"I didn't break it in the first place."

"I know. But neither did Mrs. Fetzer."

"These people are going to learn someday that I can't fix everything the vandals destroy."

"It got pretty drafty without her window."

"I suppose. H?"

"Mr. Odell says his hot water heater doesn't work."

"He's nuts."

"I know he's nuts, but that's a separate issue."

"Meaning what?"

"Meaning (a) he probably is legally insane. Meaning (b) that his hot water heater doesn't work."

"Do you know how much those cost these days?"

"Do you know how much a hassle it is taking a shower in cold water especially when you're in your eighties?"

"Just ducky. They don't want me to make any money in this place, do they?"

"Would you like to know about I?"

He sighed again. "I suppose they need a roof or something."

"I is fine."

"Really?"

"Really."

"How about J?"

"J is the Randalls and they've still got the same old complaint."

"They're the ones with the dishwasher."

"Right. The dishwasher that doesn't work," I said.

"Just tell them to give me a little time."

"Mr. Banister, they've been waiting a year and a half."

"These people just have no conception of what things cost."

"Right," I said.

"What about K? Still empty?"

"Afraid so. I'm talking to a nurse from St. Luke's Hospital. Just split from her husband and needs a place fast. She seemed to like what she saw, except all the hanging doorknobs sort of scare her a little."

"I told you to fix those."

"I'm not a handyman, Mr. Banister. I told you that when I took the job."

"Then what do I pay you for?"

"You don't pay me. You give me half my rent free for handling all the complaints and making sure that everybody stays reasonably pacified. In a way, it's a glorified security job."

"There are plenty of people who would like this position if you don't."

"Not when they add up the number of muggings, stabbings, and break-ins that go on in this neighborhood in a single month."

"Yes, and it's people just like these tenants of mine who are committing all those crimes, too."

"Mr. Banister, the average tenant here is sixty-five years old. You don't find many muggers that age."

"Well, no matter how old they are they manage to scare the hell out of my wife. She was telling these friends of ours the other night that everybody who lives here looks like one of the living dead."

"Tell her I thank her for the kind words."

He flushed. "Not you, Mr. Walsh. Not you. The others."

I sighed and stood up. "You're running late, no use keeping you."

He smiled, trying to ease some of the anger. "They just have no conception of what I have to spend on this place. No conception at all." He clucked and moved to the door. "You're doing a good job, Mr. Walsh. I didn't mean to imply that you're not. I like having an ex-detective managing my place. Makes me sleep better at night. And I should tell you that goes for Cindy, too. She was telling some of her friends at the country club all about you the other night. What a dependable man you are."

"I appreciate that."

"I'm sorry we got a little testy today."

"We get a little testy every day," I said.

"I suppose it's part of the job."

"I suppose."

Two minutes later he was in his red BMW and headed off to where people who wore saddle shoes preferred to live. He'd forgotten to ask about the other apartments, but there hadn't been anything to report anyway.

I turned back from the parking lot just in time to see the bald, eighty-one-year-old Mr. Odell standing on his second-floor balcony giving the finger in the general direction of the departing BMW. "He's a sissy bastard," he called down to me.

"You get back inside, Mr. Odell. You forgot to put your shirt on and it's thirty-six degrees." In typical Iowa fashion, what had been an Indian summer day was now gray and cold.

"He's a sissy bastard," Mr. Odell repeated and went back inside. He had not only forgotten his shirt, he had also forgotten his dentures, thus somewhat spoiling the effect of his wrath.

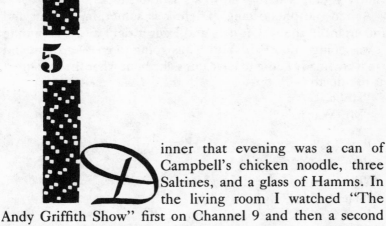

5

Dinner that evening was a can of
Campbell's chicken noodle, three
Saltines, and a glass of Hamms. In
the living room I watched "The
Andy Griffith Show" first on Channel 9 and then a second
episode on Channel 3 from Chicago. It was one of Sharon's
favorite shows and now it's mine. I'd like to get up some
morning and walk down a sunny street and stop in at the
barber shop and have Floyd cut my hair while Barney regaled
me with tales of how he conquered reluctant women and bold
criminals. Then maybe Andy, in that calm way of his, could
tell me why I spent so much time feeling anxious and depressed. If Andy didn't know, who the hell would?

The phone rang three or four times, but it was never Faith.
Twice it was people trying to sell me things and once or twice
it was tenants with questions. But no Faith.

At nine on the American Movie Classics station a Gregory
Peck movie called *The Gunfighter* came on. I was glad I was
alone. This particular movie has always had the embarrassing
ability to make me cry. I remember the first time I saw it
back in the fifties when my two boys were young. There I
sat in the Palace Theater with the lights coming up and tears
in my eyes. The boys both looked at me and then at each
other, and for the next two days it was all they talked about.

How Dad was sort of sniffling at the end of the movie. Gregory Peck gets killed at the end by the western equivalent of a snotty young bastard who wears saddle shoes.

At ten the phone rang. There was something urgent and important in the way it rang and I got it right away, assuming it was going to be Faith and I was going to go over there and we were finally going to have our talk about what she'd learned at the doctor's.

"Hello."

"Mr. Walsh?"

"Yes."

"This is Mrs. Pennyfeather."

"Oh. Hello."

"I'm sorry to be calling so late."

"That's fine."

"I'm afraid something's come up."

"I see."

"I wondered, in fact, if you could come out here."

"Out to your house?"

"Yes."

I hesitated. "Mrs. Pennyfeather, I just don't think it would be a good idea."

She hesitated. "Circumstances have changed, Mr. Walsh. I really don't know whom else to turn to."

"Did something happen?"

"Nothing I'd care to go into on the phone. Nothing I *can* go into on the phone."

"Where do you live, Mrs. Pennyfeather?"

"Out near Bever Park. Off Grande." She gave me the address. "You're coming, then?"

"I'm still not sure this is a good idea."

"This afternoon, when I met you again after all these years, I sensed you were a decent man."

"Thank you."

"I'm sorry I left so abruptly."

"That's all right."

"It's just been such a trying time for me."

"I'm sure it has, Mrs. Pennyfeather."

"I'm really rather desperate, Mr. Walsh."

I sighed. "I suppose I could come out there for a little while."

It was an odd time for it but she started crying then. Very softly. "I'm sorry, Mr. Walsh, I just feel so alone."

"That's all right, Mrs. Pennyfeather."

"You know how to get here, then?"

"Yes. I'll need half an hour."

"Fine. I'll see you then. And thank you. Thank you so much."

In the bathroom I brushed my teeth and shaved and took quick stock of my six-one, one-ninety body. All my life my baby face had been something to joke about and something that had kept me from feeling as rough and tough as I'd wanted to. Rough and tough guys just didn't have baby faces. Now, at my age, the face was something to be thankful for. When I kept my weight down, as now, I looked ten years younger than I should have. In the bedroom I put on a pair of red argyles, a white shirt, black slacks, cordovan penny loafers, and a gray wool sportcoat. I went back into the bathroom and ran a comb through my soft white hair. I kept it short, almost in a crew cut, which seemed to make it for some reason seem less old-mannish. The final touch was the Old Spice, which I slapped on with a certain ferocity. I hadn't forgotten that Mrs. Pennyfeather was a damn good-looking woman.

In the living room, just under the framed portrait of JFK that Sharon had bought on a trip to New York the year she'd died of a heart attack, I lifted the receiver and dialed Faith's number. Finally, I had an excuse to call her. I would be going out and just wanted to check in with her.

The phone rang ten times before she picked it up.

"I know it's you, Walsh."

She hadn't said hello or anything.

"I just wanted to see how you were doing," I said.

"It's just easier right now if I'm alone."

"All right."

"I know I'm overreacting."

"You have to handle it the way you handle it, Faith. There's not any right or wrong way."

"Thanks for saying that."

"It's the truth."

"Maybe we could have breakfast tomorrow morning at Country Kitchen."

"I'd like that."

She paused. "I called my mother tonight."

"How'd it go?"

"She was drunk."

"Oh. I'm sorry."

"When I told her she started crying and carrying on. Just what I was afraid she'd do."

"Maybe you shouldn't have called her."

"She's my mother."

"She's also the woman who ran off and left you before you were fifteen years old."

"She's always been an alcoholic. She couldn't help it."

"I guess."

"You've never liked her, have you?"

"Not much."

"She can be very sweet when she's sober."

I had long ago tired of the subject of her mother. "I have to go out. That's why I was calling."

"Out?"

"A case. Sort of, anyway."

"At this hour?"

"I know."

"When will you be back?"

"Few hours, probably."

"God, I didn't realize how secure I felt."

"About what?"

"About knowing you were just sitting there by the phone. Waiting for me to call. It was really something I depended on."

"It's not like I'm going to Des Moines."

"Still."

I laughed. "Maybe I could get a walkie-talkie."

She laughed, too. "You should've seen Hoyt tonight. He let Sam get up in his lap and they sat there for a long time and watched the Road Runner." Sam was their tabby cat.

"I should be back here around midnight or so."

"I'm sorry. I just have to work through this stuff."

"I know."

"Maybe I'll call you around midnight."

"I'd like that."

"Take care of yourself, Walsh."

"Right. See you."

6

The Pennyfeather house was ı Grande near Bever Park. Even in the sullen, rainy darkness it looked like a pleasant and prosperous home for pleasant and prosperous people, one of those huge old amiable white houses with green shutters and gables and even a captain's walk. Easy enough to imagine shiny black Model T's parked out front and the clink of horseshoes being pitched out back.

Three cars were parked in the driveway: a new Cadillac, a Lincoln Town Car, and a blue Volvo. I thought of how anxious Mrs. Pennyfeather had sounded on the phone. Had she panicked and called in other people to help her, too?

I pulled up under bare elm branches dripping silver rain and went up to the door.

The laughter drifting out from the living room startled me. I don't know what I'd been expecting exactly, but certainly not laughter.

I glanced around a chinaberry bush into a living room dominated by a huge fireplace with a sculpted mahogany mantel, fawn-colored matching couches that faced each other across a mahogany drop-leaf coffee table, and three different walls of French doors. Three people sat on each couch. Between them on the coffee table was a cake with innumerable glowing candles, all the more effective because the rheostatic lights had been turned low. The fireplace glowed, too, with a treated log that pulsed slow blue flame.

I wondered if I had come to the wrong place. Perhaps next door . . . . But just then Mrs. Pennyfeather came through one of the French doors bearing a bottle of champagne. Her smile matched those of the others, and her own soft laugh gathered with theirs.

I knocked.

She did the following in pantomine: She glanced to the right, where the front door was, she made a dramatic gift of the champagne to a beautiful girl in a blue dress who could only be her daughter, she leaned over and kissed the slender man who was her husband, and then she waved a delicate hand in excuse as she moved backward to the front door.

It was still several seconds before she reached it. I inhaled the fresh cold air, then exhaled, watching my white breath in front of me. A neighbor's dog sounded lonely in the long night.

The door came open with a quick *whoosh* and there she was, looking younger than she had earlier today. Perhaps it was the dark strapless cocktail dress or the way her hair was swept up on the side with a small rhinestone comb caught perfectly in the sweep of it.

She surprised me for the second time tonight. Instead of inviting me in, she came out onto the small porch and said, "Thanks for coming."

"You sounded pretty scared on the phone." I nodded inside. "But you're having a party."

"I don't suppose this is anything I should admit, Mr. Walsh, but I'm very good at hiding my feelings. I had to learn that, all those years George was—away."

I shrugged. "That seems fair enough, Mrs. Pennyfeather. I'm just not sure why you wanted me here."

In the shadowy porch light, her expression changed abruptly. She rubbed naked shoulders cold in the dark wintry chill. "Would you follow me please?"

"All right."

We went to our right, so we wouldn't have to walk past the front window. The grass was soggy from the rain, the night scented with dog droppings. "Those darn dogs in this neighborhood," she said. "We don't even have one and yet we have a yard full of—" She let the sentence drop.

The house was more massive than I'd realized, an imposing structure with an overhang roof and a vast screened-in porch on the back where you could imagine Japanese lanterns and fireflies suspended in the velvety night air.

In the back was a two-car garage recently repainted and re-roofed, the shingles gray and shiny in the gloom. Mrs. Pennyfeather may have wanted for companionship and dignity while her husband had been away, but she had obviously not wanted for money.

There was also a gazebo, one of those small but fastidious replicas of band-concert gazebos you used to see in the back yards of the wealthy. Like the garage, the gazebo was many decades old, but it had been kept up with paint and shingles and what appeared to be new latticework. It floated like a dream on the sloping back lawn.

As I approached the gazebo, curious, she put a small gentle hand on my arm. "I'm going to have to do something here I may regret."

"What's that, Mrs. Pennyfeather?"

She looked up at me. "I'm going to have to trust you, Mr. Walsh."

Now I was not only curious but vaguely apprehensive, too. My stomach tightened. "I'm afraid I can't agree to anything unless I know what we're talking about, Mrs. Pennyfeather."

"Just take a look first. Then we'll talk. All right?"

I sighed, thinking better of what I was about to do. She lifted a frail arm and pointed to the gazebo.

I walked through wet grass down the sloping curve of earth to the structure. Ground fog played at my ankles. A quarter moon was beginning to emerge behind the drizzle and the puffy gray-black clouds. The lonesome dog three or four houses away still sounded lonesome.

In shadow, I stepped up into the white gazebo, bringing enough weight to bear that the old wood creaked and let off a scent of damp rotting boards that no amount of paint could disguise. In the cold wind and rain it gave off the aura of summer dying in autumn.

It was then I saw the woman.

She was easily enough found, a heavyset, dark-haired woman in a cheap tan trenchcoat, hosed thick ankles in cheap black pumps. Next to her an imitation black patent leather purse had sprayed its contents of lipsticks and powder case and cigarettes and used Kleenex like a cornucopia smashed against a wall. She appeared to have been flung into the swing of the gazebo, a blooming rose of sopping red blood discoloring the matronly heave of her chest.

From the jacket pocket of my sportcoat I took the small flashlight I always carry with me and put the light on her face.

She had used too much makeup, her face the puffy texture of an aged doll, the lips too red, the eyebrows too black, the eyes hard blue and drained of life, like diamonds from which the color had somehow been sucked.

From habit, I bent down and began playing the flash to the left and right of her, looking for any of the obvious things you hope to find at a murder scene. Later, when the people from the laboratory got here, they would search for those minuscule clues that cheer overworked county attorneys. For now, I wanted the blind-luck items, the cigarette of foreign make, the footprint left perfect in the mud, the murder weapon itself.

Nothing; nothing.

I didn't hear Mrs. Pennyfeather come up behind me. She said, "I don't know who she is."

"Was," I said. "Who she was."

"Oh, yes. Was."

"When did you find her?"

"About an hour ago."

"She was out here?"

"Yes. Just where you see her."

"What were you doing out here?"

"I had gone to the store for some extra ice cream." She pointed to the garage. "On the way back, I cut through here to the back door. I thought it would save some time."

"You're freezing," I said.

She had begun rubbing her shoulders again, hunching into herself.

"Why don't you go inside and get a jacket?"

"Then they'd know something was wrong."

"They're going to know anyway."

"I wanted to talk to you first. The thing I'm least worried about right now, Mr. Walsh, is catching a cold."

I took off my sportcoat and draped it over her shoulders. Her flesh felt distractingly good, even covered with rough little goosebumps like the surface of a cat's tongue.

I put the light back in the face of the dead woman.

"Wouldn't it be horrible?"

"To be murdered?"

"To be murdered—and to have two people standing above you. Not even knowing who you are. It's so—impersonal. At least her loved ones would be crying and mourning her. We don't even care about her, really. She's just a nuisance, not much else."

"Nuisance?"

"Of course. Whom do you think the police will suspect, Mr. Walsh?"

I paused. "I see what you mean."

"They'll go right to George. He was convicted of murder once. It wouldn't be all that difficult to convict him of murder again."

"I suppose you're right. But there's a reason she's here."

"Oh?"

"It's unlikely the murderer killed her in your back yard by coincidence."

"You're ruling out coincidence? My father was a big fan of Stephen Crane's. Have you ever read Crane?"

"Some."

"He believed in a completely random universe. Everything was chance and accident. No God. Just the randomness and the blackness."

I turned off my light. I didn't want the dead woman's face to burn itself into my vision the way a drowning victim's once had. She'd been ten and pig-tailed and a rotted purple by the time two fishermen found her. For weeks after I would sit in my sons' room just watching them sleep in the darkness, trying to protect them, though against what exactly I hadn't been sure.

"How many people are inside?"

She thought a moment. "Seven including myself."

"How long have they been here?"

"Let's see—the first arrived about six o'clock; the last one about seven-thirty, I suppose. Why?"

"Because it's at least a possibility that one of them killed her."

For the first time, she let me see her considerable anger. "You happen to be talking about my husband, my two children; my husband's former boss and his wife and his brother. Hardly the type."

"That isn't what the police are going to say."

"You're alluding, I suppose, to my husband."

"I'm just telling you how the police are going to view it."

"The same way they viewed it the first time—that you viewed it the first time, Mr. Walsh—that George was guilty?"

Before I had a chance to say anything, a vague yellow yard light cut through the darkness collected here beneath the bare maples and elms of the back yard. A confident young man's voice said, "Mother? Mother, are you out there?"

"Over here, dear." To me, she whispered. "My son, David."

He came down from the screened-in porch, a tall young man in a tan sweater and well-pressed dark slacks. He was clean-cut in the way of a stockbroker, and except for his eyes he seemed open and friendly. Even in the shadows you could detect some troubled quality in his gaze. He carried a bottle of Heineken in his right hand and a single potato chip in the other. He came across the wet grass in an amiable stride that faltered only when I stepped down from the gazebo and he saw that his mother had a companion.

"Hello, David," she said. "This is Mr. Walsh."

He did not like me and did not particularly try to hide that fact. "In case you've forgotten, Mother, there's a party inside for Father."

"Oh, I haven't forgotten," his mother said. "It's just—"

"Why don't you go back inside and I'll talk to Mr. Walsh. I'd like to know what he's doing here."

"We seem to have a problem," I said, already tired of his attitude.

"Oh," he said, "and just what would that be?"

If he had been a little less arrogant, I might have spared him the shock tactics. But he wasn't and I didn't.

I raised the flash and turned it on the dead woman's face.

"My God," David Pennyfeather said there in the cold darkness near the gazebo. "My God."

7

"Do you have a family lawyer?" I asked Mrs. Pennyfeather.

"Yes."

"I'd call him after I call the police."

The son was still visibly disturbed. "You know what the police are going to think, don't you?"

"I know," I said. "But the longer we put off calling the police, the worse it's going to look for him."

"Would you—go inside with me?" Mrs. Pennyfeather asked me. "Perhaps you would call the police for us?"

"Of course."

David said, "Do you want me to stay out here—with her?"

"I don't think it would be a bad idea," I said, taking his mother by the elbow. "Thank you, David."

"It's all right. I understand." Those were his first civil words to me.

We went back across the wet moonlit-lawn, the neighbor's dog starting in once again, the wheels of a car splashing through the street out front, romantic music playing low, as background, coming from inside. Just as we reached the back door, she paused and took off my sportcoat and handed it back to me. "George has always been the jealous type." She tried to smile but couldn't quite.

We went in through a big shadowy kitchen that smelled of spices and out into a wide dining room. A long formal dining table with a silver candelabra in the center glistened from scrupulous polishing over the years. The lighted candles cast a soft tan glow in the room.

At the table sat three people, a prosperous-looking man and woman who were dressed up properly, he in an expensive blue double-breasted suit, she in a black evening gown with a gigantic diamond brooch riding her bosom. Lisa Penny-feather said, "Nedra and Paul Heckart, I'd like you to meet Mr. Walsh."

The couple looked puzzled. Who was I? What was I doing here? Every one of their social instincts said I didn't belong here. I put out my hand. Heckart, who had to be in his early sixties, grabbed on with an almost painful clasp, one that said despite white hair, a bit of jowliness, and a certain air of country-club indolence, he was still a strong and purposeful man.

Mrs. Heckart took my hand, too, though it was a brief social touch and nothing more, nothing to prove in it. Despite the twenty extra pounds that encased her, you could see that in her time she'd been a good-looking woman, bright of gaze and teasing in a pleasant womanly way of rich, full mouth.

The third person was a younger, trimmer version of Paul Heckart. He spoke with a certain secretiveness into a mobile phone. The way he squirmed in the chair, the fist he clenched and unclenched on the table, spoke of a deep anxiety. I wondered if it could have anything to do with a dead woman in the gazebo swing. He glanced up at me with frank resentment. I was an intruder. The Heckart brothers ran a locally prominent interior design studio for the carriage trade. They were just as snotty as you'd expect them to be.

He said, "Well, Donna, he's your husband. If you don't feel he needs to go into detox for treatment, then I guess I won't bother trying to help anymore." He spoke not in anger but instead with a certain weariness. "I'd better be going now," he said into the phone. He clicked off the connection by pushing his thumb into a button. Shaking his head, he said, "Office problems. They never end.

"It's no use, Paul," he said to the man across from him. "We've done all we can now. About all that's left to do is let him go, I'm afraid."

"God, I hate to do that," Paul Heckart said, sounding genuinely sorry.

Lisa Pennyfeather leaned forward, putting a hand on the man's shoulder. "Richard, this is Mr. Walsh."

"Nice to meet you," he said, not sounding happy at all. He didn't offer his hand. He sat there in open-necked white shirt and blue blazer looking something like a clothing ad. His silver hair lent him a sophistication his rough blue gaze denied. He was one of those seemingly pampered men whose violence always surprised you. I'd had to arrest my share of rich drunks over the years and while the majority tried to bully you with their connections, there was still a good number who were every bit as given to biting, kicking, and punching as the lowest derelict.

"I have to tell you something," Lisa said.

They sensed the urgency of her tone right away. They watched her carefully.

"I'm afraid the night's been rather ruined."

She couldn't find the words.

I leaned in and said, "Mrs. Pennyfeather found a dead woman in the gazebo out back."

"My God," said Paul Heckart.

"A dead woman?" asked Richard Heckart, trying to absorb what I'd said.

"Poor George," Mrs. Heckart said.

"We're going to have to call the police, of course," Mrs. Pennyfeather said.

"Of course," Nedra Heckart said.

"Would you mind staying here a minute or so? I'm going into the front room and speak with George and Carolyn."

"Of course," Paul Heckart said.

We went into the living room. On one of the fawn-colored couches, seated as close as lovers, sat George Pennyfeather and his daughter, Carolyn. In a blue frock with white lace at top and wrists, she was most obviously her mother's daughter, fetching and gentle in the flickering reddish flames of the fireplace.

Her first impulse was to cock her head curiously, something her mother did quite often, and say, with the soft earnestness of someone far younger, "Hello, Mother. Father was just telling me about your first date."

Her mother offered a sad smile. "Oh, that was a disaster. I'm surprised he even wants to talk about it. I was so prim."

"A goody-goody," Carolyn said, laughing. "And you still are."

My eyes moved to the small man next to her. You see them all the time, the mismatched couples, the man drab, the woman beautiful, and you wonder how and why they ever got together. George and Lisa Pennyfeather were like that, George being short, slender, with thinning gray hair, wire-rimmed eyeglasses, a baggy cardigan sweater, a dull red shirt beneath, and the slightly distracted air of a man who is more alive to internal demons than anything he sees in the material world. He sat slightly slumped, prison-ashen of pallor, offering little smiles that attached to nothing, just a nervous habit, probably, from surviving the wiles of the penitentiary. Seeing him now, I remembered spending three months on the investigation twelve years ago. He'd been like that then—quiet, pained, apologetic. One night, following two hours of intense questioning, he'd said, "I suppose all this is as much a burden on you as it is on me." He'd seemed concerned about me in some way and I'd never forgotten it, the oddness of such a reaction to a man who was trying to arrest you for murder.

"Hello, Mr. Walsh," he said now.

"Hello."

At mention of my name, Carolyn Pennyfeather turned toward me, her eyes filling instantly with anger. "Mr. Walsh?" she said. "What are you doing here?"

I didn't know what to say.

"He's going to help us," Lisa Pennyfeather said gently.

"Help us? Help us with what?" Carolyn Pennyfeather asked. "Help us ruin our evening with Father?"

Now that she was standing, I saw that she, like her brother, stood at least a foot over her parents. She had her mother's good looks, but she also had an assertiveness new to the Pennyfeather lineage.

"I don't want him here, Mother. I don't want him here at all." I put her age at a few years younger than her brother. She was probably twenty-four or twenty-three.

"I'm not trying to ruin your night," I said.

"I—I asked him here," Lisa Pennyfeather said.

"What, Mother? You invited him here?"

"Something's happened."

George Pennyfeather put his palms flat on the cushions of the couch and pushed himself to his feet. Prison had made him old. He took Carolyn's arm. "Honey, Mr. Walsh was only doing his job when he arrested me. Why don't we listen to what your mother has to say?"

I wanted him to be angry, to hate me for all I represented. It would have made a lot more sense to me, and it would have made me feel a lot less guilty. The longer I looked at this forlorn little man, the more difficult it became to imagine him a killer. Then or now.

"There's a woman in the gazebo," Lisa Pennyfeather said.

"A woman?" Carolyn asked. "What woman?"

"We don't know. That's why I asked Mr. Walsh out here. To help us figure out how to handle it."

"Handle what?"

"She's dead, Carolyn. Stabbed."

"What?"

George Pennyfeather's eyes turned ever more inward. He sat back down on the couch, slowly, as if it might be the last act of his life. He looked up at me. "It's starting all over again, Mr. Walsh."

I had to say something for everybody's sake. I could no longer be detached in the way I wanted to be. I said, "I'm going to help you find out what happened here tonight, George." I glanced at Lisa Pennyfeather. "But now I'd better call the police."

"They're going to arrest me, aren't they?" George Pennyfeather said in a dazed voice from the couch.

The strength I'd attributed to Carolyn Pennyfeather went quickly enough. As Lisa showed me to the phone, I saw Carolyn go over to a plump armchair, sit on the edge, and break without inhibition into little-girl tears.

8

"So you came out here because she asked you to?"

"Right," I said to the detective named Gaute.

"Kind of strange, don't you think?"

"Me coming out here?"

"Sure. You put her husband away."

I shrugged. "I suppose."

"You mind going over it one more time?"

"Nope."

He turned on a battery-operated recorder he carried in his pocket. He put it close enough to kiss, identified who he was and who I was and what we were talking about, and then said, "You want me to read you your rights?"

I shook my head.

"Go ahead."

"Lisa Pennyfeather called me earlier this evening."

"What time would that be?"

"Approximately ten."

"All right."

"She said something had happened."

"You know Mrs. Pennyfeather?"

"Somewhat. When I was a detective I worked on a case involving her husband."

"A case?"

"A murder case."

"I see. Continue."

"Plus which, she came to my office earlier today."

"Do you mind telling me why?"

"She wanted to hire me."

"Hire you for what?"

"To prove that her husband was innocent."

"Of the murder you arrested him for?"

"Right."

"So what did you do?"

"I declined."

"Why?"

"I felt uncomfortable. Plus I still believe he was guilty of the murder."

"Tell me about tonight."

"I arrived here about ten-thirty. Mrs. Pennyfeather came out on the front porch and led me around to the gazebo."

"How did she seem?"

"Her mood, you mean?"

"Yeah."

"Very calm. I mean, given what she was going to tell me."

"So you saw the woman on the swing?"

"Yes."

"Did Mrs. Pennyfeather know the woman?"

"She said not."

"How did Mrs. Pennyfeather explain finding the body in the first place?"

"She said she'd gone out for ice cream and put the car in the garage when she got back and had to pass the gazebo. That's when she saw the woman."

"Why didn't she see the woman on the way out to the garage?"

"That's a good point."

"You can't answer it, though?"

"No. You'd have to ask Mrs. Pennyfeather."

"How did the people inside react?"

"About the way you'd expect. Shock. Disbelief. Carolyn, the daughter, seemed to take it hardest of all."

"How about Mr. Pennyfeather?"

"He's afraid you're going to blame him for the woman's death."

"Did he say why he thought he'd be implicated?"

"Well, he's only recently been released from prison for one murder. He gets home and a few days later an unidentified woman is found in his back yard. Dead. Anybody would get nervous."

"So nobody inside the house said or did anything that might lead you to think they had something to do with the murder?"

"No."

He shut off the recorder. He was a tall, chunky man in a tan all-weather coat and a snappy gray fedora spattered with raindrops. He smoked a cigarillo with a white plastic tip, and he smelled of Aqua Velva. He was probably fifty. "You got any thoughts on it at all?"

"Not really."

"You don't find it strange she called you?"

I thought about it. "I find it strange, yes. But I don't think she set me up or anything."

"You base that on anything in particular?"

"No," I said. "I think she found the woman and got scared."

"So why did she come to your office this morning?"

I saw what he meant. It did seem awfully coincidental. I looked out at the back yard. It blazed white with lights from the county men doing the medical exam and the lights from Channels 2, 7, and 9. Down some of the white latticework on the gazebo you could see a few lurid splotches of red blood.

"I guess I should talk to Mrs. Pennyfeather a little more," Gaute said.

He put the recorder back into his coat pocket. In profile, his silhouette against the lights in the back yard looked broken and tough. "It all looks pretty strange right now. By morning things should be a lot clearer."

"There's a positive mental attitude."

He smiled. "They gave you that crap, too, when you were working for the county?"

"Sure. They had these psychologists come in every year or so and try to pump us up."

"You see a kid get run over, you just got to keep it in perspective. That kind of stuff."

"You got it."

"What a crock that stuff is."

I laughed. "It doesn't help you a lot when you're really down, that's for sure."

He tipped his hat toward me, starting to make his move to the back yard. "Those shrinks?"

"Yeah?"

"They're crazy. Every one of them."

He went down the steps and into the explosion of light that had made the ground soggy brown, the trees flat black, and the gazebo the drab gray color of all things that die in winter.

9

I sat in a room filled with a Baldwin baby grand and several bookcases packed with the book club editions of the past decade's bestsellers. A floor lamp, burning low, made everything shadowy and melancholy.

This was another half hour past the time I'd spoken to Detective Gaute. Through louvered windows, I could see where the police had roped off the front of the lawn to keep onlookers out. The ambulance gone, the crowd was beginning to thin. In the rain the onlookers had the soaked fervid air of religious zealots awaiting a miracle. It was unlikely the dead woman was going to come back from the grave.

I had wanted to say goodbye to Lisa Pennyfeather. Now, seeing that my watch read past midnight, I wanted only to get home. I'd tried Faith's number. The line was busy. I knew what that meant. Whenever she was upset, she took the receiver off the hook. I'd tried the operator just in case. She checked the number and said that there was apparently a problem with the line. She said she'd report it. I said not to bother.

So I sat now with a slick magazine called *Country Home*, staring at pictures of a rambling rustic home Sharon would have loved, leaning into the soft glowing warmth of lamplight and letting my eyes close every few seconds in drowsy bliss. Not unlike Faith, I sometimes dealt with problems by sleeping through them. Unfortunately, I had learned this trick only a few years ago. Before then I'd been given to pacing and cigarettes and coffee liberally laced with whiskey.

In the back yard you could hear the wind in the darkness and then the police and officials moving around in the light-blasted night. Every once in a while there would be a laugh, and in the silence of this small, handsome room the sound seemed vulgar and out of place.

I must have dozed. I heard my name called softly. When I got my eyes opened I saw that the door had been closed, and before it stood the beautiful daughter Carolyn.

"Mr. Walsh?"

I sat up, setting the magazine back on the stand.

"This is sort of embarrassing," I said. "I must have been asleep."

"I'm the one who's embarrassed."

"Oh?"

"For treating you the way I did."

I smiled. "Believe it or not, I've been treated much worse."

She came from the shadows in the circle of light. She was her mother thirty years ago, floating on the generational tide. "I've hated you for so many years now, I'm shaking." As evidence, she showed me a small, well-turned hand. It trembled.

"I would have hated me, too."

"But you were only doing your job. Somehow I didn't realize that until tonight."

"If a man had helped put my father in prison, I would have hated him, too."

She came closer into the soft shadowy light, an anxious animal. Until now, she'd kept her left hand behind her back. Now, she brought it around. It held a white envelope. She leaned forward and gave it to me.

"I'd like you to take this," she said.

"What is it?"

"A check for five hundred dollars."

"For what?"

"I want to hire you."

I slumped back in the seat, unreasonably tired and already hating myself because I knew what was coming, and because I was going to refuse her. "As I said to your mother this morning, I just don't think it's a good idea."

"He knew her."

"I beg your pardon?"

"He knew her. My father knew the dead woman."

"Oh."

"You heard what he told the police?"

"No."

"He told them that he'd never seen her before and had absolutely no idea who she was."

"That wasn't smart. They can check."

"They can and will. That's why I need to hire you."

"Your mother wanted me to prove your father was innocent of the first murder. Now you want me to prove that he's innocent of the second as well?"

She put her hands primly in front of her. The Pennyfeather women had a way of making primness most erotic. "They're connected."

"The first murder and the second?"

"Of course."

"You know that for a fact?"

She shook her head. "But common sense would say so."

"Common sense doesn't get you very far with the law. Not unless you have some sort of evidence to back it up with."

"Think about it. He hasn't been out of prison a week and here a woman is murdered in his back yard. Somebody decided he would be the best candidate for a—well, a frameup, as melodramatic as that sounds."

"He was framed for the first murder and now he's been framed for a second?"

"Don't scoff."

"I'm not scoffing. I'm merely being properly skeptical. It's something to be skeptical about, don't you think?"

"You know my father. Do you really think he could kill anyone?"

"Sometimes the meekest of people become the most savage of killers."

"Well, that may be so. But not my father."

"I don't see how I can help."

"Check on the woman. Find out whom she knew and what she had to gain from my father."

"Why are you so sure he knew her?"

"Because I saw them together yesterday at Ellis Park."

"You did?"

She nodded. "Yes. I was following him."

"Your father?"

She stared at me with her huge luminous eyes. "It sounds terrible, I know. But each afternoon since he came back he'd go off somewhere by himself, and when he'd come back he'd seem very upset. I asked him about this but he wouldn't say anything. He said he just liked to drive around and enjoy his freedom. But I knew better."

"You didn't hear anything they said?"

"No, I wasn't that close. But I did look in her car and copy down her name and address. They're in the envelope." She looked off into the gloom of a darkened corner. "He's so sweet. So gentle. He has been all our lives. He— Well, you can see how beautiful my mother is. I don't suppose you'd expect her to marry a man like my father. She was obviously pursued by so many more handsome men. But they didn't have any of my father's quiet charm or his dedication to being a husband and a father." She turned back to me, her eyes shiny with tears. I saw her mother again in her face and heard the whisper-soft sorrow in her voice. "There's nobody else I can turn to, Mr. Walsh. Nobody else."

I got up and put my arm around her and she came into my embrace and I held her while she cried. She moved with soft frenzy as she pressed against me. The door opened, and her mother came in and saw us. "Carolyn!" she said. "Honey, what's the matter?"

Carolyn turned from me and started to compose herself.

I said, "She just hired me, Mrs. Pennyfeather."

"Hired you?" Lisa Pennyfeather asked. "But I thought—"

I laughed. "Nobody could resist two Pennyfeather women. Nobody."

"Well, at least looks still count for something in this world," Lisa Pennyfeather said. At another time it would have been a wry observation; now it just sounded forlorn, particularly since it was accompanied by thunder rumbling across the mid-night sky.

I said goodbye and was pulling away from the curb in less than a minute and a half.

10

On the way home there were a few snow flurries. They made the night seem darker and more endless, and inside my car, the heater roaring, I felt isolated, as if I were trekking along across an infinite and unknown prairie. Drunks from taverns weaved home on foot, angled against the bitter wind and flurries. The closer I got to my apartment house the more patrol cars became evident, a teenage driver stopped here, an aged black man with empty eyes and a shabby topcoat stopped there.

The Alma's parking lot was filled. My spot, clearly marked Manager, was empty. Sometimes I'd come home late, find something there, decide against hassling the residents to find out whose car it was, and park three blocks away, the closest parking area.

Lights shone in only two of the fifteen units as I made my way up the sidewalk to my apartment. The flurries were becoming real snow now. I stood outside my door letting the snow hit my face and melt. I even stuck my tongue out so a few flakes would land there. The first snow always makes me revert to childhood; over on 10th Street S.W. I was the first kid on the block out with my Western Auto sled, even if only a few flurries had been spotted. I smiled at the memory. So many decades ago. It seemed impossible—and even more impossible that the boy of that memory had anything to do with the man who stood here now, all these long years later. There were going to be a lot of different me's crowding that coffin when the time came.

With the door only halfway opened, the first thing I noticed was the smell, the unmistakably pleasant odor of eggs, hash browns, toast, and coffee.

When I got in and closed the door, she came out of the kitchen, an apron tied around the waist of her forest-green shortie robe, a spatula in one hand and a glass of clear liquid in the other. The liquid would be vodka. She liked to drink it straight and warm. She was one of those people who got mildly drunk on two stiff drinks and then coasted on the buzz the rest of the evening.

"You want to go in and kiss Hoyt?"

"Sure."

I went into the bedroom. In the moonlight I could see Hoyt in his blue jammies with the feet. She had him carefully propped between two pillows so he wouldn't roll off the double bed. I went over and bent down and kissed him. His face was warm with sleep. He breathed as if he were slightly plugged up with a cold. Sometimes, like now, I just closed my eyes and held him tight. At these moments I knew he was mine and knew that however thorny my relationship with Faith, she'd given me my life's last important gift. I touched his plump, warm little cheek with my fingers and pulled the covers up to his chest again (Hoyt was a hell of a kicker and could strip his bed in twenty minutes just by rolling around). I plumped his pillows, making sure they'd keep him from falling off.

In the kitchen, she said, "I should get him baptized."

"I'm not pushing."

"You're a Catholic. You know you want him baptized."

"I tried to call you earlier."

"Had the phone off the hook."

"How you doing?"

She looked at me. Her red hair slightly mussed, her green eyes red from crying earlier, she said, "Fair."

"You must be doing better than fair."

"Why?"

I grinned. "The food. Looks like you're going to feed a baseball team."

"Oh. Right." She sounded slightly dazed. "I woke up in my apartment. It was real dark and funny."

"Funny?"

She nodded. "You know how you wake up and you always hear cars going by on Second Avenue?"

"Uh-huh."

"Well, I woke up and I didn't hear anything. It was as if— as if I'd died. It was very dark and there wasn't any sound at all."

I took two steps toward her. I was tall enough to tuck her into my arms. I held her just that way for a long time, closing my eyes as I had with Hoyt. I'd always assumed that because of my age, the first death we'd have to face together would be my own. All that was changed now—at least potentially.

"The bacon," she said.

"The hell with the bacon."

She started crying. "At least turn it off, would you?"

"Sure."

I went over and turned it off, then took out the eight strips and laid them on the double fold of paper towel she'd laid on the counter. I daubed the excess grease off with the towels and then put the strips on a white china plate.

I went back to her and put my arms out but she said, "I guess I just don't feel like being held any more." She looked at me and kind of shrugged. "I'm sorry." She glanced at the eggs and the bacon and the toast popped up in the silver four-slice. "We should eat."

"You really feel like eating?"

"I don't want to waste the food. It's your food."

"I'm not worried about the food."

"I could try to eat."

"I wish you would."

She ate three eggs, four strips of bacon, and two pieces of toast that threatened to disintegrate under the weight of all the Kraft grape jelly.

"I'd hate to see what you'd do if you ever really got hungry," I said.

She stuck her tongue out. "Very funny."

We sat at the drop-leaf dining room table in the living room, the table I'd bought Sharon right after World War II, the table at which my boys had eaten while growing up. They were fathers themselves now, one in California and one in New Hampshire. I'd turned on the small light on top of the TV and opened the blinds so we could see the snow. It was coming hard and big and fluffy now, and it was going to stick. If it had been just any other night when Faith and I were getting along, it would have been wonderful to sit here and feel animal-snug and animal-warm sheltered from the cold and snow.

She said, "They've scheduled me for a mammogram the day after tomorrow. You know what that is?"

"Yes. Where?"

"Mercy."

I sipped coffee. "You didn't tell me what the doctor said. At least not exactly."

"I'm sorry about this morning. I was pretty freaked out." Then she smiled. "God, 'freaked out.' I haven't said that since 1968."

"That's all right. I still say 'scram.' I don't believe anybody's said that since 1939."

" 'Scram'?"

"Ummmm."

"I had an uncle who used to say that."

"He probably wasn't your favorite uncle, though."

She smiled. "I guess he wasn't."

"So what did the doctor say?"

"He said that 80 percent of the lumps found in women's breasts are noncancerous. They're filled with fluid and called cyst-asperate. A lot of these the doctor can check right in his office. By touching the lump, he can generally tell how well defined the edge is, how close to the surface it is." She had a quick hit of her vodka. "I wasn't that lucky. About him being able to tell right in his office. He said he just couldn't be sure."

"That isn't necessarily bad news."

"I know. I'm just scared."

"Does breast cancer run in your family?"

"Two aunts. One survived it, one didn't."

"This could all be about nothing."

"I know."

"Your babysitter Marcia said her cousin Rosie turned out to be all right."

"Isn't she great? Marcia, I mean." She was never more enthusiastic than when she was describing a woman she liked. She'd had problems with men all her life—too beautiful for some, not beautiful enough for others, though I found that unimaginable—and as a consequence she spoke with pure delight about women and with great guarded skepticism about men. Then, "You mind if I stay here for a while?"

I grinned again. "Honey, I've been asking you to move in with me for a year. Why would I object now?"

"I guess I didn't figure you would."

"Anything you need, you just tell me."

"All right." She paused and looked at me. "There's something I should tell you."

She used a certain tone whenever she was about to tell me something that would hurt me. She used that tone now. "I've been seeing somebody."

"All right."

"Kind of seriously, I mean."

I nodded.

"Seriously for me, anyway. He's the usual rotten jerk. He even hit me once. He gets real jealous and—I don't know what to do."

I could feel my jaw start working.

"You know how I told you once that sometimes I need you to be my lover and sometimes I need you to be my father?"

I cleared my throat. "I remember."

"Well, for a while anyway, I need you to be my father. Do you mind?"

"No, I don't mind."

"I mean, I'm not going to see this guy. I really want it to be over with."

"All right."

"But I don't feel like—well, you know, making love or anything. Can you handle that?"

"Sure."

"And I'm really scared so I'm probably going to be kind of bitchy to be around. Will that be okay?"

I laughed. "Yeah, I sure haven't ever seen you bitchy before."

She reached across the table and put her hand on mine. "God, I really do love you. You know that?"

I slept on the side of the bed with the nightstand in case the phone rang. I had a tough time getting to sleep. Hoyt rolled over against me and I just held him small and warm against me and looked out the window at the snow in the yard light. Faith went to sleep pretty fast, snoring softly and wetly in the darkness. Just as I started to drift off, Hoyt's considerable little fist bonked me on the nose hard enough to make me tear up. Then I teared up for real and lay there cold and scared. I said a Hail Mary for Faith. I hoped Hail Marys still applied in the modern world.

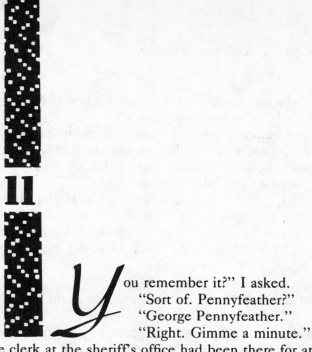

11

"*Y*ou remember it?" I asked.

"Sort of. Pennyfeather?"

"George Pennyfeather."

"Right. Gimme a minute."

The clerk at the sheriff's office had been there for at least twenty years. As a consequence he remembered me, and there was at least a chance that he remembered the Pennyfeather case. I needed to look through the files before I got anything serious accomplished, which was why, twenty minutes after breakfast with Faith and Hoyt, I'd come down to Mays Island, where you find the new Linn County sheriff's building, the Linn County courthouse, and, on the far end of the island, the Cedar Rapids municipal building. The island divides the city in half. Early in Cedar Rapids history the island provided a home for various types of reprobates, including horse thieves and the homegrown version of pirates. Now things are a little more respectable, though I've known some lawyers who hang out at the courthouse who are not necessarily any better than the reprobates of a century and a half ago.

At dawn the snow had stopped, leaving an inch of powdery whiteness that a strong southeasterly wind was blowing away from car windshields and roadways. The sky, framed in the window of the office where I sat, was low and gray. The day's drabness hadn't helped Faith any. She's one of those people who live at the mercy of weather.

While I waited, I smoked a cigarette and looked around at the orderly row of filing cabinets, the General Electric clock radio with the minute hand that no longer swept, and the clean glass ashtray I was about to violate.

He came back in, crisp in his tan uniform and his narrow bald head, sat down behind his desk and said, "Oh, yeah. Right. George Pennyfeather." He skimmed through the pages and said, "He killed this Jankov because he thought Jankov was sleeping with his wife."

"Right."

"And you were the detective in charge of the case?"

"Right."

"How come the Cedar Rapids boys didn't get involved?"

"The killing took place in a fishing cabin out near Ely. County matter. Though they assisted."

"Oh. Right." He looked through a few more papers. "Murder weapon was a .38, never found."

"Mmmhmmm."

"Witness put Pennyfeather at the cabin fifteen minutes before the shooting." Riffling through additional papers. "Never pleaded guilty to a lesser charge."

"Apparently he thought he could beat it."

"Or knew he was innocent."

"Thanks for the vote of confidence."

He looked up and smiled, revealing a gold-capped tooth. "Sensitive bastard, aren't you?"

"I suppose."

"He's back in the news."

"Yeah."

"Dead woman in his back yard."

"Yup."

"I assume he's under suspicion."

"I would think so."

"You going to read this file here?"

"Right."

"I can't let you make copies or anything."

"I understand."

"And all the offices are filled at the moment so you'll have to sit right here."

"Okay."

"I usually walk over to that bakery across the bridge and get a roll. Takes about fifteen minutes in all. Wife makes me because of my weight."

"Yeah, and having that roll probably helps your weight out."

"It isn't a big roll."

"Now who's being sensitive? I was making a joke."

"Cigarettes."

"Huh?"

"I gave up the cigarettes and I put on twenty pounds in the first three months and I still can't get rid of them."

"Maybe that's why I don't quit."

"Well, I'd rather have a gut than lung cancer."

"I guess you've got a point there."

"Also a hint."

"Huh?"

"I wish you wouldn't smoke while you read the file."

"Oh. Right."

"Stuff just hangs in the air and gets into my hair and into my uniforms. Can't stand the smell of it anymore."

He pushed the manila file at me and stood up. "Well, time for my walk." He went over and got a green parka that was part of the uniform. "Good luck."

"Appreciate it."

"You want me to bring you a roll back?"

"I had a good breakfast."

"That's the hell of it."

"What is?"

He zipped up the parka. The noise was louder than you might think here in the quiet of this back office. "I had a good breakfast, too. Now I'm going out after another one."

He gave me something that resembled a salute and left.

12

They were never rich or fancy houses, the ones that stretch out Ellis Boulevard along the river, but after the war and well into the sixties they were the kind of sturdy middle-class homes people I knew wanted to live in. I'm not sure when it changed, when the new Chevrolets and new Fords and the occasional sparkling Pontiac became rusted-out metal beasts that seemed to be dying of some disease . . . but change it did. The people with good factory jobs moved out, up into the hills, or out into the dense housing development along O Avenue, or over near Edgewood Road where young doctors and other professional people were starting to give the west side a good reputation again. Leaving Ellis Boulevard to the ravages of the night. Oh, occasionally you saw new shingling on a house, or a new roof, or a spanking new paint job, but mostly—smashed windows, junk overflowing on porches, a dead car on the front lawn—mostly the area was sliding into slow and certain death now, hanging on for another generation until the urban renewal monster came along and gobbled it up, decimating the Timecheck area so completely, all trace of its existence would be gone forever except for a few fading photographs in Grandma's photo album or the civic history section in the library.

She lived in one of the worst houses. According to the radio reports, the police had now identified her as Stella Czmek, age forty-eight, unmarried. The reports offered no information about what she'd been doing in the Pennyfeathers' back yard in the first place.

From a beauty shop on the corner came two fat black women. One had plump pink curlers in her hair, the other what appeared to be an almost comically long cigarette dangling from her mouth. Seeing what house I was standing in front of, they frowned at each other and whispered a few things. As they drew near me, the lady with the curlers nodded to the house where Stella Czmek lived and shook her head with a slow sadness.

"Hello," I said.

The woman with the cigarette nodded. "You any relation to Stella?" she asked.

"No. I'm afraid not."

"You heard what happened to her, didn't you?"

"I sure did. Terrible. You knew her, then?"

The lady in the pink curlers had a very pretty face buried in excess flesh. "Not real well."

"She didn't like black people much," her friend said.

"Especially us," said the woman in curlers.

"Why not you especially?"

"Oh," she said, " 'cuz one day we was walking past her porch and she flipped her cigarette just so it'd about hit Dolores here. Right on purpose."

"Absolutely on purpose," Dolores said.

"So I told her, right then and there, I said, 'Lady, in case you think you're any better than we are, you just take a look at this house you live in.' "

No doubt about her point. In a long row of dirty gray houses in various stages of falling apart, Stella Czmek's had been one of the grimiest, rust stains like blood running down the filthy white shingles around the small porch.

"What'd she say to that?" I said.

"Called us 'nigger trash,' " said Dolores.

"Bitch," said her friend.

"That was about it, huh?" I said.

"Till about two weeks later, when she got that car."

"Oh, yeah," said Dolores. "You should've seen that car."

"Big?" I said.

"Big ain't the word for it." Dolores giggled. "Try humongous. Right, Esther?"

"Cadillac?" I asked.

"Lincoln," Esther said. "You could sit in the front seat and on this little panel you had controls to do everything."

"Lock all the doors, roll up all the windows," Dolores said. "Everything."

"It was her car?"

"That's what she said."

"She had money, then?"

Inevitably, Dolores looked at Esther. A tiny frown appeared in the corner of her mouth. She looked back at me. "Are you the police?"

"Nope."

"A friend of hers?"

"Not that, either." I took out my wallet and showed it to them.

Dolores was positively ecstatic. "Just like Mike Hammer on TV!"

Esther pulled the license I was holding toward her. "I'll be damned. I never seen no private eye's license before. This for real?"

"For real."

"The cops was here all morning," Dolores said. "Asked everybody in the neighborhood stuff about her."

"Didn't get much, though," Esther said. "Either people didn't know her or they seen what she was like when she was drunk and they didn't want to know her. And that goes for white and black people the same."

"She drank a lot?"

"Oh, my, did she drink," Esther said, giggling again. "I mean, I maybe shouldn't be sayin' this about her, her just dyin' and all, but she was the worst drunkard on the block. And believe me, there's some champion winos on the block. Some *champions*. See that little grocery store down there?"

I looked down the block. A shabby little place of smashed windows and 6-PK Beer $1.99 signs stood on a corner across the street from the beauty parlor.

"Four times a day," Esther said.

"Four times a day?" I asked.

"That's how many times she'd make a trip to that store."

"She drank beer in the quarts. She'd get two a trip. Plus cigarettes if she needed 'em," Dolores said.

"She have any friends?"

Dolores nodded to the house next door. "Mr. Bainbridge, he talked to her sometimes." She rolled her eyes. "In his line of work, of course."

"What's he do?"

"Well, what he does and what he *thinks* he does is two different things."

"Oh?"

"What he does is work at the post office sortin' mail. But what he thinks he does is minister to our needs." Dolores laughed. "He got hisself some degree from some bible college in Texas and ever since then he walks around thinkin' his shit don't stink. Excuse my French."

"So he was trying to save her soul?"

"Tryin'," Esther said sardonically.

"What time does Mr. Bainbridge get home?"

"Usually about three-thirty. But he's home right now. Seen him 'bout an hour ago peekin' out from behind that curtain right up there. He was watchin' the police."

"Wonder why he's home," I said, hoping one of them would volunteer an answer.

"Beats me," Dolores said.

"You gettin' cold?" Esther asked her. "I'm gettin' cold and I'm headin' inside."

"Real nice meetin' you," Dolores said.

"Likewise," I said, and gave each of them one of my business cards.

"You a private detective. I just can't get over it."

I smiled and watched them walk down to the end of the block. They waved to each other and went into separate houses, the grave dignity of the womanhood sad counterpoint to the wry girlishness of their laughter.

When I looked up, I saw a pair of eyes behind thick glasses peering from behind burlap curtains and out of morning gloom. The eyes behind the heavy lenses stared down at me from the second floor. As soon as we made eye contact, the curtain flapped shut.

The two-story house had been painted chocolate brown many decades ago. The brown showed everything—dust, mud, rust, even the white undercoating where the shutters over the front window had been torn out and now hung loose. On the porch were stacks of aged newspapers, yellowed and winey with the odor of mildew. Over the doorbell was a small cracked decal of the American flag. Another decal, this one on the small glass pane of the door itself, said, This House Protected by Jesus and Smith and Wesson.

I rang the bell and leaned forward to make certain it rang. It didn't. Inside I heard the noises of an old house settling, and then quick, sharp footsteps on the staircase. I peered into shadow so deep it was virtually like nightttime. All the curtains were drawn.

He opened the door so abruptly, I took a step back, sensing he might attack me.

He was skinny, tall, with an almost grotesquely large Ad-am's apple, short-trimmed gray hair, pasty white skin, eyeglasses so thick they seemed comic, and blue eyes that spoke of turmoil, grief, and abiding madness. He was probably a few years younger than me. In his plaid work shirt and baggy jeans and house slippers, he looked like the sort of melancholy psychotic you saw roaming the halls of state mental institutions just after electroshock treatment, the pain and sorrow only briefly dulled by riding the lightning.

"I saw you talking to those nigger women," he said. It was an accusation.

I had my wallet ready and showed him my license.

"What's this?"

"Private detective."

He glared at me. "Private detective?"

"Yes."

"About what?"

"I'm trying to find out some things about the Czmek woman."

"Why?"

He used his short, pointed questions the way a boxer uses jabs—to keep his opponent off balance.

"I'm just trying to find out some things about her."

"For who?"

"I'm afraid I can't say."

"You came to the wrong place."

"You didn't know her very well?"

"No."

I stared at him and sighed. "Mr. Bainbridge, all I want is—"

"It isn't 'Mr.' "

"No?"

"No, it's 'Reverend.' "

"Oh. Excuse me. Reverend."

"Inside I have a degree that says I'm a reverend."

"I see."

"But don't think I'm gonna help you just because you call me by the right name."

"All I want is—"

"I know what you want."

"You do?"

"It's obvious."

"It is?"

"You want to know if we ever fornicated."

"I do?"

"That's what those nigger women were telling you."

"Oh?"

"Don't play innocent."

"That doesn't happen to be what they said."

"I don't believe that. They used to spread stories about Stella and me all the time."

Just by referring to her as "Stella" he confirmed what Dolores and Esther had told me.

"How's your ministry doing?"

"What?"

"Your ministry. How's it doing?"

"I suppose you're really interested."

"I am. You said you were a minister. Seems a logical question to ask, how your ministry is doing."

"You know darn well what they did to me."

"They?"

"The people down on E Avenue. At The Church of Jesus Praised."

"I'm afraid I don't."

"Sure you do. That's another lie those two nigger women love to tell."

"About The Church of Jesus Praised?"

He nodded. " 'Bout that teenage girl and how I was supposed to've been peekin' in that hole and all. They just said that to get rid of me 'cause I wasn't afraid to say they was preachin' the Devil's gospel." He leaned forward, as if church members might be standing behind me on the porch. His blue eyes glanced about with birdlike speed. "Reverend Cahill is the Antichrist."

"Really?"

He pulled back into the doorway and nodded. "That's why they put that hole in the wall. So I'd look inside just out of idle curiosity. I didn't know no fourteen-year-old girl was goin' to the bathroom in there."

"And as soon as you peeked in that hole—"

"They landed on me. They was just waitin'." Bitterness curled his lower lip. " 'Course, they told the police that I put the hole in the wall."

"And the police believed them?"

"They're part of it."

"Part of what?"

"Part of the Antichrist's plan. Who do the police protect today?"

"I guess I'm not sure."

He swelled his chest up slightly and fixed me with a long bony finger out of which he probably imagined a death ray was firing. "Today the police protect niggers and drug dealers and queers. Those are the people who will run this country once the Antichrist has taken over."

"I see."

He eyed me carefully. "You're not a believer, are you?" He was back to making accusations.

"Not in the way you mean."

"You go to church?"

"Sometimes I go to mass. Not very often, I'm afraid."

"Mass," he said, chewing the word as if somebody had just put a turd in his mouth. "You know about the pope?"

I sighed. "This the one about how he has sex with nuns all the time or the one about how he's secretly Jewish?"

"Sarcasm is the Devil's device."

"Look, Reverend," I said, tiring of his madness and no

longer able to sustain my pity. He'd be better off shot dead, I thought, despite all my Christian training. His grief was beyond help and his viciousness was dangerous. "I'd just like to ask you some questions about Stella Czmek."

"All I'll say is that she was my friend."

At least this was an improvement over pretending he scarcely knew her.

"Did she come into some money?"

"What's that supposed to mean?"

"I'm told she suddenly started driving around in an expensive new car."

He glared down the street to where Dolores and Esther lived. "Can't keep their mouths shut, can they?"

"You know where she got the car?"

"No."

From the wallet I took a twenty. Before coming over here, I'd driven into Merchants Bank out on Mt. Vernon Road, deposited the check Carolyn Pennyfeather had given me, and taken five crisp twenties from the automatic teller machine.

One advantage a licensed investigator has over a cop is that he can bribe people. In the kind of world we live in, that's one hell of an advantage.

I held the twenty out to him. He looked snake-charmed by the sight of the bill.

"I'd like you to take this."

"Why?"

"Call it a contribution to your ministry."

"I ain't gonna tell you nothin' about Stella."

"Here. Please."

I could see him weakening. In a way, it was almost disgusting.

"You ever ride in that car of hers?"

"What if I did? We never fornicated, no matter what those nigger women said."

"It have a nice radio?"

"Very nice."

"I'll bet those nice plump seats were comfortable."

"Real comfortable."

"And those electric windows."

He grinned and I saw the boy in him. The boy looked just as screwed up as the man. "They was fun to do."

"Who do you think gave her the car?"

"Oh, no."

"Pardon?"

"Oh, no. That's what you want, ain't it?"

"What is it I want?"

"That fella's name. The one who come to see Stella sometimes."

"Well, I certainly wouldn't mind if you—"

"Oh, no." He pushed his hand up, almost knocking the twenty from my fingers. "You just go on, git out of here."

"But Reverend—"

"You just git and git fast."

He slammed the door as abruptly as he'd opened it, the sound booming off the snowy gray morning.

At least I'd learned that Stella Czmek had had a friend who was worth trying to track down.

13

On First Avenue, near St. Patrick's, I found a drive-up phone and pulled up. For my quarter I got to talk to a female voice who identified herself as the cleaning woman and who told me that none of the Pennyfeathers were home. I asked if she could tell me where they'd gone. She sounded reluctant. "Some things came up," she said.

"I'm a friend of the family's."

"Oh."

"So you'd be doing both them and me a favor by telling me where they went."

"I really don't think I should say anything." She paused again. "They went—" She stopped again. "I'd like to hang up now, if you don't mind."

She didn't wait for an answer.

Sitting in the car, the wind cold through the open window, I took what was left of the phone book (it appeared that some deranged beast had taken out all its anger on it) and looked through the yellow pages for the number of David Pennyfeather's law office.

After the receptionist identified the place, I said, "I'd like to speak to David Pennyfeather, please."

"I'm afraid he's unavailable right now."

"Is he in?"

Hesitation. "Yes."

"Thank you."

Because his office was only six blocks away, in the center of the downtown area, I decided it was worth driving over. I made one more phone call and left.

Following the recession of the early eighties, Cedar Rapids decided to impose its will on an unfriendly economy. Despite factory closings, long free-food lines, and some bad national publicity, the city gambled on its own future by turning the downtown into a model of refurbishment. Buildings that appeared to be on the verge of desertion were torn up and rebuilt with a ferocity of purpose that unsettled a good deal of the electorate until they finally saw the transformation completed—tall, gleaming buildings; skywalks; rebuilt offices that bore no resemblance to their former crumbling selves. It used to be easy to stand on the corner of Second Avenue and Third Street, say, and imagine how, only a few decades earlier, farm wagons used to roll into town on Saturday mornings bearing sweet little girls in braids and grinning little boys with wide eyes. Cedar Rapids was then a center for all the surrounding farm towns, but now it was a center for much more—national and international business alike. The restoration had been successful in all respects, as the bumper-to-bumper Mercedes-Benzes and all the fast-walking yuppies proved. The blueplate luncheon at the Butterfly used to cost $1.25. Now you could easily drop twenty times that in several of the more fashionable spots. Now it was almost hard to imagine that farm wagons had ever rolled down these streets.

David Pennyfeather's office was on the third floor of a building that had once been a department store. Not that you could tell.

I rode up on the elevator with two young women who carried briefcases and smoked cigarettes with an urgency that said they weren't able to indulge upstairs. They were mysterious creatures to me—attractive without doubt, but aggressive in the way men were aggressive, angry and curt, sarcastic and bitter. I had no doubt that they were a lot tougher than the men from whom they still probably had to take orders.

A massive wooden door meant to impress gave the Trotter, Styles and Pennyfeather law offices the air of a fortress under seige. I put my hand on a doorknob that seemed far too frail to open such a formidable door, and pulled.

Everything was mahogany and leather except the carpet and drapes, which were a sedate red the color of dried blood. In a wooden alcove, bent over a computer screen, was a spiritual sister of the two women in the elevator. Her auburn hair caught in a soft chignon, her knit dress an impeccable and dazzling white, the receptionist seemed to know vast and consequential secrets I couldn't even guess at intelligently.

Disappointment registered quickly in her brown eyes. She probably didn't see many clients dressed in car coats, white shirts, and chinos. "May I help you?"

"I called a few minutes ago about seeing David Pennyfeather."

"I'm afraid he's still busy."

"Would you tell him Mr. Walsh is here? I was at his parents' home last night. He'll probably remember me."

She let her irritation show. I was doing two things wrong. One, I wasn't taking her hint that I should just leave. Two, I was taking her away from her work at the computer screen.

She stood up. "If you'll have a seat over there, I'll go speak with him."

"Thank you."

She nodded and left the reception area. If her body wasn't perfect, it sure came close, tall and lean in a worked-at sort of way. One thing I've got to give my sons' generation. They take care of themselves. Physically, anyway.

First I looked through *Forbes*, and then I looked through a two-day-old *Wall Street Journal.* I had no idea what I was reading. Mostly, I looked for cartoons. *The New Yorker* was a lot more fun to skim through.

I sat in a fat leather chair long enough that one of my legs started to go to sleep. I was stamping my foot, trying to get some circulation going again, when the receptionist came back.

Standing over me, she said, "He can give you a few minutes."

"I appreciate it."

"He's very busy." She was scolding me, angry that he'd agreed to see me at all.

"Thanks again."

She led me down a carpeted hall. Behind various closed doors I heard the rumble of male voices being earnest. On the walls were Grant Wood reproductions. When I was young, I could never understand why Wood painted the way he had. One day when Sharon and I were on a picnic, though, I stood on a hill just outside of Anamosa and looked down at the blue vein of creek and the green roll of hill and the gathered brown of forest and then I saw it, saw just what Wood must have seen, and ever since, all other nature paintings have seemed slightly wrong to me. He got it right and he was the only one.

David Pennyfeather was waiting for me. He wore a three-piece gray suit and black horn-rim glasses. For all his size, he looked like a mean boardroom version of his mother. He was perched on the edge of his large mahogany desk. His office looked just like the reception area, only smaller.

I put my hand out. He shook it without enthusiasm and broke quickly. "Why don't you close the door, Mr. Walsh."

"All right."

I went and closed it and came back. I glanced down at a chair. He held up his hand. "You won't be here long enough to sit down, so don't bother." He put his hand out palm up. "I'd like the $500 back that Carolyn gave you."

"Isn't that between Carolyn and me?"

"Hardly. Carolyn, much as I love her and much as I respect her intelligence, can be very naïve."

"Have you ever considered the fact that I may be trying to help her?"

"To be honest, no. You're a retired cop who runs a nowhere apartment house. I checked you out, Walsh. Personally."

"Did you check far enough to see that I'm a licensed private investigator?"

"If I wanted to hire an investigator, Walsh, I'd hire one of the reputable ones. There's a Pinkerton office as close as Des Moines. For just one example."

"You seem to forget. You didn't hire me. Your sister did."

"Well, I'm just helping her out. Actually, you saved me a trip by coming up here. I talked to Carolyn this morning and she expressed some misgivings about hiring you. I told her I'd take care of it."

"I don't believe that."

"I don't give a damn what you do or don't believe, Walsh." He narrowed his eyes into a practiced gaze. He got up from the desk and pushed half a foot toward me. I had no doubt he was a tough man. He was bigger and younger, and I wasn't stupid. "You were the man who arrested my father. The whole idea of hiring you is ludicrous."

"Your mother doesn't seem to think so."

"My mother's been so hurt and confused she no longer knows what to think."

"So you'll do her thinking for her?"

"That's right, Walsh. That's right."

He went back around his desk and sat down. "We're through now." He put his head down. Apparently my audience had ended.

"Where's your father?"

"Did you hear me? We've finished talking." He kept his head down.

"When I called, the cleaning woman said that something had happened. She wouldn't tell me what."

"It's none of your business."

"Maybe I could help. You've got a nice mother and a nice sister. I've even started to like your father."

"The same man you helped put in prison for twelve years, even though he was innocent?" He let his anger go. It was considerable. He looked miserable now, young suddenly, and frustrated. "Just get the hell out of here, all right?"

I decided to have one last go at it. "You didn't advise him to hide, did you?"

He said nothing.

"That's the sense I got from the maid. That your mother had taken your father someplace. That wouldn't be smart. You know the police are going to want to talk to him."

He sat back. His gaze softened somewhat. "How would you react? You just get out of prison and all of a sudden they're threatening to take you back again. And both times you were innocent."

"Running isn't going to help."

He put his head down again. "They're not running. They're just trying to figure out what to do." He looked up. "Now, goodbye. Do you understand? Goodbye."

I put my hand on the door and let myself out.

Twenty minutes later, parked on Second Avenue, I watched as David Pennyfeather came quickly out of his building. He wore a gray overcoat and a black fedora. He moved without pause.

I followed him to the Second Avenue parking ramp. I waited below. It took five minutes before he appeared again in a new blue Volvo sedan.

He was upset enough that he nearly rear-ended a truck stopped at a light. He was also angry enough that he started leaning on his horn, as if the truck driver was at fault. The driver gave him the hi-sign and then spent the rest of the red light shaking his head about the condition of the human species in general today.

David Pennyfeather moved straight down Second Avenue and across the bridge, at the end of which he took a left.

After another near-accident, this time with a white-haired old woman in a big battered Buick, he clamped both hands on the wheel and began driving with real determination.

Ten minutes later we were on a gravel road that led to the interstate.

We were going out of town somewhere.

14

Snow was more obvious in the hills where the horses ran, large white patches of it over the land brown with winter, and on the roofs of the farm houses that hugged the land sloping up to the timberline. Even on overcast days the land holds a severe beauty, milk cows plodding the fallow fields along the fencing, farmers tossing handfuls of yellow feeder corn to hogs like nuggets of gold, the fat lone snowman in the front yard with a green John Deere cap tilted across its eyes of coal, clean winter wind whipping in the bare black trees on the edge of a hill.

David Pennyfeather took the Amana exit, going west as soon as he reached the arterial highway, a two-lane strip of blacktop that skirted the original Amana colonies where the black-clad locals had until a few decades ago rolled back and forth to town in heavy farm wagons and buggies.

I hung back a quarter mile, afraid that he might get suspicious. At a sandy road veering sharply off the highway, he took an abrupt hard right. He must have known the road reasonably well because he didn't slow down at all, taking the first turn around a stand of firs at sixty miles per hour.

When I reached the same spot a few minutes later, I saw that below this road ran another, a narrow, angling devil that led deep into a forest of pines and high red clay cliffs. If he suspected I was following him, he could easily pull off the road, stop his car, and wait for me in a blind.

I had no choice but to go ahead.

Ten minutes later, coming to a stop on the edge of a clay cliff, I saw finally where he was headed.

Below lay a cabin on the edge of the river. In summer, when it was surrounded by blooming trees, you would not be able to see the place. Even now it was hidden behind a wind-break of pines. I'd sighted it only because I'd seen the blue of his Volvo flashing on the other side of the trees as he pulled up to the cabin.

I backed my car off the road, locking everything up, and got out. From here I'd have to do everything on foot.

The first thing I checked was the cliff. It was a sheer drop and I didn't think I could make it down that way. At my age you minimize your risks.

I took the road, which was little more than a winding dirt path that allowed for one car to pass. Arced across the gray sky was a silken pheasant enjoying itself now that hunting season was over. Just around the bend that pitched down to the cabin a fox glanced up from its feast of a dead squirrel, eyeing me cautiously but not threatened enough to move. My feet crunching tiny pieces of ice, I finished the rest of the walk with my collar turned up, a pair of green earmuffs riding my head. My nose felt like an ice cube.

The cabin was a large and fancy affair, built of logs to give it a rustic look but enhanced with housing shingles on the roof, a small satellite dish, and a screened-in porch large enough to seat at least a dozen people comfortably. In addition to the blue Volvo there was a new Cadillac Seville, in dark papal colors, and a small silver Porsche.

There was no point in trying to sneak up and eavesdrop. The best way in was the most obvious way. I went up to the screened-in porch and opened the door, walked across a floor covered with dark green indoor-outdoor carpeting, and stepped over to the front door. There was a large black gas grill on the far side of the porch. You could still smell the summer's burgers.

I knocked.

Instantly, you could hear voices cease their talking, and *shush*ing sounds being made as they tried to figure out who was on the other side of the door.

Moments later, David Pennyfeather appeared.

"What the hell are you doing here?" he asked when he saw me.

I looked beyond him to where his mother and father stood in the center of a large room with a beamed ceiling, next to a fireplace crackling with pleasantly smoking logs, a tall stack of which lay next to me near the front door.

"I wondered if I could speak with you a minute, Mrs. Pennyfeather," I said, ignoring David entirely.

He shoved me hard enough to push me halfway back across the porch.

His mother and father shouted for him to stop. They came running. Carolyn, taller than anybody in the family except David, seemed to appear from nowhere and grabbed David's shoulder. "Stop it!" she shouted. "Right now, David! Do you understand?"

"He followed me!" David said.

George Pennyfeather, small and quiet, said, "Let him come in, David. He's only trying to help."

David Pennyfeather took three threatening steps into the porch. I could see now how bad his temper was. He was having a difficult time getting control of himself. From the weary pleas of his family, it was also easy to understand that they'd had to deal with his anger for many years.

Carolyn Pennyfeather pushed herself ahead of him on the porch. She slammed her hands flat-palmed against his chest. For the first few seconds he managed to push her back but then she dug in with surprising strength and slowed him down considerably. "You stop it, now, do you understand? Do you understand?" She might have been talking to a dog she could no longer control.

Knowing there was no way I could hold my own in a fight with him, I'd picked up a log, wielding it as impressively as possible. He didn't even seem to notice.

"Why the hell did you follow me?" he said. He was still angry, but he was no longer acting irrationally.

Carolyn, still between us, said, "Let's invite him in and sit down and talk. All right, David? All right?"

You could see him collapse inside his expensive gray suit. Miserably, he said, "He's your problem, then, Carolyn. And you deal with him."

She looked back at me anxiously and said, "I will, David. I will. Now you go back in there and sit down. And right now. Right now."

He glared at me once more and went back inside.

15

hope that's warm enough," Lisa Pennyfeather said fifteen minutes later.

"It's fine," I said.

"I hope I didn't put too much lemon in it."

"I'm sure it'll be just right."

Carolyn laughed, her gentle, beautiful face regal and sad. "This is what I call Mother's 'hostess anxiety.' She can never relax whenever anybody outside the family is in the room. She just can't sit still making sure everybody and everything's taken care of properly."

"She exaggerates," Lisa Pennyfeather said fondly, putting her small hand on Carolyn's shoulder.

"Probably not by much, though," I said. "And speaking of that, why *don't* you sit down?"

"Well," said Lisa Pennyfeather, looking at her husband and son on the plump plaid couch. "Well, I guess I should, shouldn't I?"

She sat down and lighted one of her improbable Luckies.

Roughsawn cedar boards gave the cabin's interior the proper pioneer feel. Whittled down ends gave all the boards an old-fashioned pegged look. Old brass and wrought-iron trim finished the motif. Shaggy throw rugs, wicker stands overflowing with magazines and board games, and a good deal of aged but comfortable furniture made me wish I lived here.

"This is a very nice place," I said.

"We all like it," Carolyn said. "Except David." She sat on the arm of the armchair David filled. She poked him playfully. "You never have liked this place, have you? Not even when we were kids." She looked at me and smiled. "He really is just as crabby as he seems, Mr. Walsh."

After a few minutes of seeming relaxed, David appeared uncomfortable again. Not angry; melancholy. There was a sense of real gloom about him as soon as she'd mentioned the cabin.

George Pennyfeather, cleaning his eyeglasses with his tie, said, "I'm still very happy that Paul—Heckart—made us a present of this place that time. His interior decoration business had really taken off at that point, and he was feeling generous."

"It was on our wedding anniversary," Lisa Pennyfeather said to me. "He came over to our house with a cake and candles and then just handed us the keys. He used to let us use it all the time—and then he just gave it to us."

David, still seeming uncomfortable with the drift of the conversation, said, "This is all nice and fine to sit here sipping our tea. But it still doesn't answer the question of what he's doing here in the first place."

"David," George said. "You don't need to be rude."

Prison had neither toughened him nor coarsened him, not in any obvious ways, anyway. He sat there in his yellow shirt and blue cardigan and tan slacks and gray slip-on Hush Puppies as quiet and polite as a seventh-grade English teacher during the principal's visit to class. But of course all this could be deceptive. Many murderers are essentially shy people forced by their own desperation—perhaps by their very shyness—to strike back at a world that has always subtly punished them for not being more demonstrative.

"All right, since my family insists on courtesy, Mr. Walsh, why don't we just let you tell us why you came out here?" David said.

"To help."

"Sure," David said.

"David," Carolyn said. "There's no reason to talk like that." She nodded to me. "Anyway, as I told you, I hired Mr. Walsh."

David glowered. "Well, I unhired him."

"What?" Carolyn said.

"After you told me what you'd done, I took the liberty of phoning your bank and stopping payment on the check."

Her cheeks were tinted with anger. "You had no right to do that. No right at all."

He backed down some. "I'm sorry if I made you angry. I was only trying to help."

I said, "I wonder if you'd go for a walk with me." I was speaking to George.

He glanced at his wife. "Uh, well, of course."

"I'm sure you two have things to talk about," Lisa said. "And by the time you get back, I'll have some sandwiches fixed for you."

"See what I mean about 'hostess anxiety,' Mr. Walsh?" Carolyn smiled.

I smiled too. "She's got it pretty bad. No doubt about that."

"The worst part was the medical care. Or lack of it. I suffer from asthma, Mr. Walsh."

"I hear it's pretty bad. The care, I mean."

"Sometimes I'd have to wait days. And even then you don't always get to see a doctor. You see a nurse and if you come at the end of the day, it's even worse. She's worn-out or crabby and she makes you wish you hadn't come in the first place."

We were walking along the river. Out in the center, tugged

by the currents below the choppy dark gray water, a rowboat was being pulled downstream. A tall man in green rubber fishing gear sat with one oar in the water, letting himself be dragged downstream until he found a suitable place to cast. On the far shore the birches looked almost pure white.

A dog trotted along behind us. George Pennyfeather had already said the mutt didn't belong to him. It resembled some odd combination of huskie and collie. He'd come up every few feet and lick my hand. His tongue was warm and familiar. I thought of our boys growing up, how they'd loved dogs. Now, neither one of them liked pets. They had wives who valued clean houses over companionship.

"I don't imagine any of it was much fun, prison."

"I became religious. That helped a great deal."

I shrugged. "I suppose I would, too."

"The worst part was missing Lisa. That was the absolute worst part. I missed the children, of course, too. But Lisa— well, I've always been one of those men who needed a mother as well as a wife. And Lisa was always willing to be both."

We walked up a narrowing trail. He went ahead. He spoke to me over his shoulder. "Passing the time is the hardest part. I didn't get involved in any of the politics and I learned not to make myself available to anybody for anything. That's the fastest way to get used in prison—sexually or any other way. To make yourself available in some way." He turned and glanced ahead at the leaf-covered hill we were cresting. Then he smiled back at me. "It's a good thing I was the meek CPA type. It prepared me for surviving prison. I knew how to keep my mouth shut."

When we reached the top of the hill we stood looking down at the water bashing the rocky cliff we stood on.

I said, "Lisa still insists you were innocent."

He looked at me almost apologetically. "I know this will probably hurt your feelings, Mr. Walsh, but I was and am innocent. Just as I'm innocent of killing the Czmek woman, though my lawyer was informed that the police will charge me with her murder sometime today."

"That's why you came out here?"

"Yes."

"Running?"

"Not exactly." He tilted his head to stare down at the hard smashing water. "I just wanted some time with my family. If we'd stayed home there would have been reporters and neighbors and relatives. You know."

"Last night you said you didn't know the Czmek woman."

"Yes."

"Carolyn tells a different story."

"I know."

"I doubt she's lying."

"No," he said. "No, she's not. I'm the one who's lying."

"I see."

"I don't think you do, Mr. Walsh."

"No?"

"No. You see, once I said I knew the Czmek woman, then there would be nobody else to suspect of the murder except me. I didn't want to help the police any more than I needed to. No offense."

"Carolyn followed you."

"Yes, she told me."

"Would you tell me why you saw the Czmek woman?"

"I'm afraid I don't know."

"What?"

"I really don't. Know, I mean."

"But Carolyn—"

"Oh, I understand why she thinks what she does. If you'd followed me that day you'd have had the same impression she did. Meeting this strange woman in the park. Arguing with her. And this only a few days after I left prison." He shook his trim little head. No matter how old he got, he would always look like the precocious eight-year-old who knew how to act around grown-ups. "But I'd never seen the Czmek woman before."

"Then why did you meet her?"

"Because she called me and told me she could supply me with the evidence I needed to prove myself innocent of killing Karl."

"Did she say what this evidence was?"

"No."

"Or where she got it?"

"No."

"She wanted money?"

He smiled. "Oh, of course."

"How much?"

"Ten thousand dollars. Cash."

"Did you bring it that day?"

He raised his head to follow the flight of blackbirds against the gray sky. They were headed south. Far behind the others was a tiny fluttering bird that threatened to drop from the sky. From here you couldn't tell if it had been injured in some way or if the freezing November air currents were simply too much for it. I looked away in case it fell from the sky. I felt helpless enough already with Faith. I didn't need some little bird to remind me again of how powerless we are to help one another.

"Oh, yes, I brought it that day. Wouldn't you if you'd been given a chance to prove you were innocent?"

"Yes, I guess I would."

"Fortunately, Lisa and I come from very wealthy families. Within reason, money's never been a problem for us, or for Lisa while I was in prison."

"So you gave it to her?"

"No. There wasn't time."

"Not time?"

He shook his head.

"She saw somebody and got scared."

"Where?"

"I'm not sure. In the park, I think. Near us. She got very frightened. She said she'd call me later and just took off."

"You didn't get any kind of look at this person who frightened her?"

"None."

"Did she have time to show you any of the evidence she was going to offer you?"

"I'm afraid not."

"So then she just took off?"

"Yes."

"How long did you stay there?"

"Ten minutes. I was stunned. I'd gotten my hopes so high. So had Lisa. We'd let ourselves believe that everything was going to be all right and then—that's why Lisa hired you right after this. To help us."

"Did you see the woman again?"

"No," he said.

"Or hear from her?"

"No. The next time I saw her was in the back yard."

"Did you try to contact her?"

"No."

"How about your family?"

"My family?"

"Did any of them try to reach her?"

He turned to me, disturbed. "What is it you're trying to suggest here, Mr. Walsh?"

"I'm merely looking at all the angles."

"All what angles?"

"The police could certainly make the case that one of your family, disappointed that the Czmek woman didn't come through with the evidence, got angry and killed her."

"They don't even know about her."

"Lisa did. And Carolyn took her name from the car."

"No, it's not possible."

"Then that would leave you."

He sighed. "Yes, I suppose it would. And I'll tell you something."

"What?"

"If they're going to blame any of the Pennyfeathers, I would prefer it be me."

"That's very honorable, but the police will keep looking until they get the right one."

He smiled again, showing for the first time a vague bitterness. "The way you kept looking into my case, Mr. Walsh?"

I said nothing. There was nothing to say.

"Are you getting cold, Mr. Walsh?"

"Yes."

"Then why don't we go back. Did you find out what you wanted?"

"Yes."

"It was the Czmek woman you wanted to talk to me about?"

"Right. And turning yourself in."

"I knew you'd come to that."

"It's the best thing for you, Mr. Pennyfeather. Staying out here at the cabin sounds very nice, but it's certainly not going to look very good for you."

"I suppose not. It's just—" He shook off the thought. "I seem to have developed this aversion to correctional institutions. I'm not even sure I could enter the police department without making a total fool of myself. Every night since I've been home, I've had nightmares about being locked up again. The noise. The smells. The violence. They're terrible nightmares, Mr. Walsh."

"I'll be glad to go to the station with you. If you think that would help."

"Oh, that's all right. I appreciate the offer, though."

I watched the dog who'd tagged along lift his leg and send a seemingly endless stream of yellow urine into the grasping roots of a giant oak tree. Steam rose.

I said, looking back at George Pennyfeather, "I meant that. About me going with you to the station."

"Oh, I'm sure you did."

"You just tell me when."

He stared at me. "Are you going to keep working for my wife and daughter?"

"If you'd like me to."

"I would indeed."

"Then I will."

"What if you find out that you put the wrong man in prison?"

I stared back at him. "I'm not sure how I'd handle that. There really wouldn't be any way to say I was sorry."

He laughed softly and then put a small hand against my arm. "Carolyn said she trusted you, and by God if I don't, too, Mr. Walsh. Now that's a big surprise."

We walked back to the cabin.

16

Early in the afternoon I ate lunch in my car, Hardees being the culprit. I sat between a panel truck belonging to a plumber and a motorcycle belonging to a guy my age who still obviously remembered Marlon Brando and *The Wild One*. About this time, I assumed, George Pennyfeather would be in his lawyer's office and they would be phoning the police, arranging a time to go over to the police station. While it was not certain that he would be arrested, it was certain that the police wanted to talk to him. After being a good citizen and tossing my crumpled bag into the depository Hardees had prepared for me, I wheeled my car across the street to a drive-up phone. I let it ring twelve times before giving up. Faith and Hoyt had gone someplace. My hand tightened. I could almost feel her bed-warmth in my fingers. Faith; Faith . . . .

Most of my background checks begin at the credit bureau, and for a simple reason. In assessing a person's credit, the bureau collects all sorts of peripheral information. While legislators have debated the legality of the bureau's gathering this information, it is nonetheless just the sort of material you need when you're checking somebody out. You get a lifetime's worth of employers, any pertinent spousal information, and a

pretty good sense of how the person has been doing econom-
ically. (I've always thought that smart drug czars, for instance,
would purposely allow themselves to have a *bad* credit rating.
But then "smart" and "drug czar" are two concepts that usually are mutually exclusive.)

The bureau was busy this afternoon. A neatly dressed
woman (big floppy ties were in vogue this season) argued with
a clerk about certain things that had been left in her file. A
lawyer I recognized from the courthouse gravely pointed out
some file items to a very anxious-looking client, the lawyer
whispering a bit too loud the phrase. "Chapter 11," as in
bankruptcy. A young couple, cheery and confident and en-
viably in love, chattered amiably with a clerk about their in-
tentions to buy a little house up in the West Highlands area,
and therefore needing a Xerox of their record to take to the
realtor and to the bank.

I got the Stella Czmek file by convincing the manager that
if I didn't get it a client of mine would be in great and abiding
trouble. He let me see the file. He was used to my melo-
dramas.

She had been born in 1941, graduated from St. Wenceslaus
High School in 1959, worked for ten years at Cherry-Burrell
in the shippping department, attended Hamilton Business
College at night where she learned secretarial skills including
dictation, and had then gone to work for a man named Jerry
Vandersee, who operated an import-export business out of the
Executive Plaza building. Originally, for the duration of her
employment at Cherry-Burrell, her credit rating had been terrible. People's Bank had been forced to reclaim a 1965 Mus-
tang it had loaned her the money to buy; Standard Appliance
had sued her for money owed on an Admiral TV console, an
Admiral refrigerator, and a Tappan gas range. A revolving
charge account she'd had at Armstrongs had been cut off after
six consecutive months of nonpayment. She was evicted twice

from apartments on First Avenue West for being in arrears on
her rent. After finishing her courses at Hamilton, and after
joining Vandersee's International Import-Export, her life
seemed to improve—not right away and not as if she'd won
the lottery, but over the first year with Vandersee you saw
steady improvement in her rating. She'd rented a small house
up near St. Patrick's, started a modest savings account at
Merchants Bank, and paid $500 cash down on a 1964 Ply-
mouth. At this time she married a man named Stan Papajohn,
who was then employed by Wilson Packing Company in the
hog kill. Four months after the marriage, they moved to a
house on Edgewood Road, N.W., where they soon bought a
motorboat and successfully applied for credit cards at Killians
and Younkers department stores. This was in 1973. The marriage lasted eight years, during which time the Papajohns saw
their financial status become very, very good. There was even
money for a small lake cottage up on the Coralville Reservoir.
After the divorce, things didn't seem to go so well for either
of them. Stan Papajohn lost his job when Wilson was sold;
Stella Papajohn (who had gone back to calling herself Stella
Czmek) was unemployed for nearly two years after the death
of her employer, Mr. Vandersee. Nowhere in her file was any
mention of children. Apparently broke, Stella Czmek slid back
to her old way of life. There were several credit complaints
dating from 1982 to 1986. A 1985 Ford Fairlane was repos-
sessed by Farmer's State Bank in Marion. An eviction from
an apartment in the Calder Arms led her in 1987 to her last
address on Ellis Boulevard.

From a pay phone in the lobby, I called Stan Papajohn. A
somewhat harassed-sounding woman answered as a baby cried
in the background.

"Mr. Papajohn, please."

"Who's this?"

"My name is Walsh."

"Who you with?"

"Uh, with myself. I have a small investigative agency."

"Investigative agency?" She cupped the phone and shouted at the squalling infant to god dammit shut up. "What kind of investigative agency?"

"I do background checks."

"What're those?"

"Employers hire me to make certain that potential employees are who they say they are."

"Oh." She obviously had no idea of what I was talking about.

"Is Stan there, Mrs. Papajohn?"

"We ain't married."

"I see."

"So I'm Kitty Malloy, not Kitty Papajohn."

"Right. What time does he get home?"

"Why?"

"I'd like to talk to him a few minutes."

"About what?"

Always tell the truth, particularly if there are no other options. "I'd like to ask him a few questions about his ex-wife."

"Why don't you ask me?"

"You knew her?"

"No, but Stan and his brother Jimmy told me all about her. A real ball-buster, take my word for it. She wanted to wear the pants in the family, if you know what I mean."

"Did you ever meet her?"

"Just once."

"When was that?"

"Say, you know she's dead, right?"

"Right."

"Does this have anything to do with that?"

Once again, having no choice. I nobly told the truth. "Yes. I'm working for somebody who's involved in the case."

"Oh."

"You said you met her once."

"Right. She came over here one night, real drunk and abusive and demanding to see Stan. I didn't have no choice but to let him go with her. They went down to the Cedar View."

"The tavern?"

"Right."

"Do you know why she wanted him?"

There was a pause. "You'll take this wrong, if I tell you."

"I'll try not to."

"I don't think he told me the truth. Stan, I mean. And he never did that before. Lied, I mean."

"You're saying you don't know why she wanted him?"

"Right. Oh, he came up with some cock-and-bull story about her needing a loan, but she was always the one with the money, anyway."

"I see."

"She had some inheritance or something."

"That's what she told Mr. Papajohn?"

"Right."

The kid started crying again and once again she cupped the phone and said god dammit Ricky shut up.

"What time does Mr. Papajohn get off work?"

"Three, if he don't work overtime."

"I'd like to leave a message."

"Lemme get a pencil, Mr. Walsh."

The kid was crying. She was saying shut up god dammit as she hung up.

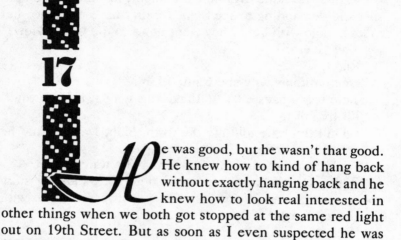

17

He was good, but he wasn't that good. He knew how to kind of hang back without exactly hanging back and he knew how to look real interested in other things when we both got stopped at the same red light out on 19th Street. But as soon as I even suspected he was following me, I started taking rights and lefts, out through the plantation-style homes along Blake, and then past the elegant houses sweeping up to Cottage Grove. You've never seen a wooded residential area any lovelier. I was going a long way out of my way and he was going with me.

I swung over to Clark Road then, and finally to Mt. Vernon Road where I quickly pulled into a self-serve car wash. If I'd done my work right, he was going to come screaming down the street any minute now, wondering just what the hell had happened to me.

He came along in one minute and forty-six seconds and boy did he look pissed.

While he was at the stop sign, looking so hard left and so hard right I thought he was going to give himself whiplash, I strolled over to his new metallic green Chevrolet and knocked on the driver's window.

He turned toward me so fast, you might have guessed he'd been shot.

The first thing he did was roll down the window. "Just what the hell do you want?"

"Directions."

"Huh?"

"Why don't you pull over into the 7-11 drive there and you can tell me where you're headed."

"Now why would I want to tell you something like that?"

"Because you've been following me for the past hour and I just thought that maybe you knew where we were going. I don't seem to."

"Get lost."

He started to roll up the window. I put my .38 right in his face.

"Hey," he said. "You pulled a gun on me."

"That seems to be the case, doesn't it?"

"What the hell are you doing?" He sounded hysterical.

"Pull over there. And don't try to move too fast. I want to walk right along with you."

"Do you have any idea how many municipal laws you're breaking?"

"Probably a lot of them."

"God," he said, still in the throes of disbelief.

I walked right along with him. I pushed my body close enough to the car that nobody could see the .38 unless they were looking straight in.

He didn't seem to be so much scared as irritated. He just kept shaking his big, bald head. He had shaved it. Apparently he still remembered when Telly Savalas was doing all right with the ladies. He was probably in his early fifties, but the aviator shades and the brown leather bombardier and the white turtleneck sweater were meant to suggest a sixth decade given over to beer-belly macho.

He pulled into the 7-11 lot on the far side where I instructed him. I told him to shut off the engine and hand over the keys.

"You're really pushing it, pal," he said. But he gave me the keys.

I walked around the car and got into the back seat. The car still smelled new.

"I'm going to have your ass busted so hard, you won't believe it," he said. He had a way of whining that spoiled his angry words.

"Who hired you?"

"I have no idea what you're talking about."

"Who hired you?" I asked again.

"I guess you're just going to have to shoot me, pal. I don't have a clue about what's going on here."

"Let me see your billfold."

"Why don't I just give you the cash? Let me keep the other stuff. Sentimental value, you know?"

"Billfold," I said.

"You muggers are getting a lot bolder, I've got to say that for you. Walking right up to my car in broad daylight."

He gave me his billfold. It was some kind of crushed black leather. I looked inside. It was right there waiting for me.

"The Conroy Detective Agency," I said.

"So?"

"You just out for a nice drive today, Conroy?"

"So what if I was?"

I dropped the wallet on the front seat. "Now let's see your log."

"My what?"

"Your log."

"I don't know what a log is."

"Right." I pushed the gun against the back of his sleek skull. "The log."

"Huh?"

"Open the glove compartment."

"Why?"

"You know why, Conroy."

"You sonofabitch."

So he opened the glove compartment and took out his log and handed it to me. It was nothing more than a small thirty-five cent spiral tablet. It had a sketchy drawing on the corner of a freckle-faced kid with a mortarboard on. As I took it, Conroy said again, "You sonofabitch."

Most investigators keep logs. It's the best way to document your driving and your expenses, not only for the client but also for the IRS boys.

Conroy stared at me in the rearview as I looked over his morning's entries.

"You jerk," he said.

"I thought I was a sonofabitch."

"You're both."

"Well, that's some kind of distinction, anyway." I handed him his log back. "Who's at 2987 A Avenue?"

"I'm sure I don't know."

"That's the address you've got written down here."

"Then it must have been by accident."

"Uh-huh. How about the other address, on Mount Vernon Road?"

"Another accident."

"You know, Conroy, when I saw you wearing those shades on a day this overcast, I said to myself, nobody could be that dumb. It must be a disguise. He's disguising the fact that he's actually very bright and in control of the situation."

"Very funny."

"But you know what I found out? You're even dumber than you look, Conroy, and that's an accomplishment, believe me."

"Can I go now?"

"You know how easy it will be for me to find out who hired you now that I've got these addresses?"

"I wish I knew what you were talking about, pal."

Now I was the one who was getting irritated. "We're probably going to meet again, my friend. And next time it won't be half as pleasant as this little routine. You understand?"

"I'm peeing my pants I'm so scared."

I glared at him and sighed. I was the one with the gun and he had me right where he wanted me.

I got out of the car. After I'd walked around to the driver's window, I tossed the keys into the front seat.

"We through now?" he said.

It was one of those times when I wished I had something smart to say, a capper to his line. But nothing came. I walked across the street to the car wash and got into my car.

Conroy took off.

18

At a drive-up phone, I called my apartment. Faith answered on the second ring.

"How're you doing?" I asked.

"I was doing pretty good until I turned on the TV. Guess what my favorite soap opera is about today."

"I don't know."

"You can't guess?" She sounded wound pretty tight.

"Faith, I'm afraid I can't guess. I'm sorry."

"Well, what am I worried about? What am I going through? I turn on the TV set, thinking my favorite soap opera will help me get my mind off what's happening to me—and guess what it's about? I mean, don't guess; that was rhetorical. I'll *tell* you what it's about. It's about Beth dying. She just learned today that she's got this terminal illness." She sounded about to cry.

"It's just a terrible coincidence is all. Turn it off and watch something else."

"It isn't a coincidence. Don't you see that?"

"Then what is it?"

"A sign."

"A sign?"

"Sure, it's a sign. It's telling me that I'm going to die."

"Oh, honey, why do you do this crap to yourself? Go play with Hoyt or just watch something else."

"Don't start patronizing me. Just because you don't believe in astrology and stuff."

"It isn't a sign," I said. "I promise."

She didn't say anything for a while. A truck rumbled by. "Where are you?" she said, sounding notably calmer.

"Drive-up phone on Mount Vernon Road."

"When are you coming home?"

"Now, I'm not sure."

" 'Now'? You mean you were sure but now you're not?"

"I was headed home when somebody started following me."

"Somebody?"

"A private investigator named Conroy."

"This sounds like a movie."

"Well, it's true. And now I've got to check out a couple of addresses I took from him."

" 'Took'? What's that mean?"

"Nothing important. I'll explain when I get home."

She was silent again. "You really don't think it's a sign?"

"I really don't."

"It's just a coincidence?"

"One time I had a real sore throat and I went to the doctor and he told me I'd better go to a specialist and have it checked. It scared the hell out of me. That same afternoon, I went to this used bookstore where I always go and I bought a detective novel, figured that would get my mind off it, a book called *Blowback*. Guess what it was about?"

"What?"

"This private eye who has to have his throat examined because he may have cancer."

"You're kidding."

"Swear to God."

"You're not just saying this to make me feel better?"

"It really happened."

"And you didn't see it as a sign?"

"No, I just saw it as a terrible coincidence."

"God, I really would have freaked. I really would have."

"Now please just go watch something else, okay? I love you, Faith, and I want you to relax. Do you understand?"

"Thanks. Really. Thanks. You're such a good man. You really are. I don't deserve anybody as good as you. I really don't."

"That's me," I said. "A real prize."

We kissed into our respective receivers and hung up.

19

The first address on Conroy's log was a white bungalow on A Avenue N.E., over in what realtors like to call transitional neighborhoods. Not too long ago you would have seen Packards and Chryslers sitting in the drives and also along the curbing. Now the cars ran to ten-year-old heaps whose rusty bumpers proclaimed how they'd visited shrines such as Graceland or Grand Ole Opry or Six Flags in Nebraska. Women of many races—white, black, oriental—dragged reluctant kids along the sidewalk, threatening to spank them or worse, while on the porches, despite the temperature, sad-eyed men without shaves or hope sat sucking on cigarettes and quarts of 3.2 beer. They were waiting for something that had long ago passed them by, and probably without them even knowing it.

The porch tilted when I stepped on it. As I approached the door, I heard whispers inside the front window, and I saw a young girl jump behind a couch. She was playing, probably at her mother's instructions, a game of hide-and-seek, the same sort she'd play when a bill collector came to call. I didn't like the feeling that I was ruining the life of a four-year-old.

I knocked confidently, as if I didn't have anything at all to hide, as if I was the most reasonable and gentle man who'd ever come to call.

This time I saw a woman in her mid-thirties pop up from behind an overstuffed chair and then pop back down. There was something familiar about her, though at the moment I wasn't sure why.

I knocked once more and while I waited moved over a few steps to the rusty black mailbox that was hanging at an angle to the door, held in place by a single nail.

Through a slot in the lid I could see the white edge of an envelope. Quietly, I lifted the lid and took the envelope out. As I'd hoped, it was mail coming in, not going out.

Her name was Kathy Stacek. I knew instantly why she'd looked familiar a moment ago. Kathy Stacek had played a key role in convicting George Pennyfeather of murdering Karl Jankov. She was the witness who testified that she'd seen George at the scene of the crime, and probably carrying a gun.

I put the envelope back, and just as I turned to go back to the door I heard the porch creak and I saw the two of them moving toward me. Obviously they'd been inside. They'd come out the back door and around front.

"What do you want?" the red-headed one said.

They were dressed similarly but not identically. Both big men gone to early-thirties beer fat, they wore chafed black leather jackets, T-shirts, faded and grubby jeans, and motor-cycle boots bulked at the toes with steel reinforcement. The redhead had more scars than the blond-haired guy. Both of them looked in need of jobs, shaves, baths, and dental work.

"I was hoping to speak with Kathy," I said.

"Kathy don't want to speak with you," the redhead said.

"You mind if she tells me that herself?"

By now they were on the porch. I'd expected an argument, some macho banter back and forth, but they surprised me by getting down to business right away.

The redhead got me by the shoulder and slammed me face first into the front door. I could taste the dry dust drifting up from the rusty screen. He got my arm behind me and bent it sharp and fast.

"Hey, Christ, Johnny," said his buddy. "Take it easy. This guy's gotta be sixty years old."

"Who the hell are you?" Johnny said, and gave my arm another sharp twist that again pushed my head into the screen door.

"My name's Walsh," I said. "I'm a private investigator."

"What the hell you doin' here?"

More pressure on my arm. I could feel the pain all the way up into my shoulder.

"I saw this address in a log."

"What log?"

"Belonging to another private investigator. Conroy."

"That's who that sonofabitch was this morning," Johnny said to his pal. "I told you, Eugene. I told you he was some kind of cop or something."

Apparently, Johnny was of the opinion that he could get back at Conroy by hurting me. I looked down the street. Nobody seemed to be paying any attention to a white-haired guy pushed up against the door while two bikers had sullen fun with him, that white-haired guy being me of course. I watched a small kid Hoyt's age in a red snowsuit. He sat perched on a small mound of dirty city snow. He was, of course, eating the snow.

Johnny surprised me. He let me go.

I spent the first thirty seconds just rubbing my wrist and forearm.

"You leave her alone, you hear me?"

"Who?" I said.

"You mess with her," Eugene said, "and Johnny's really going to lose it." He chucked me under the chin. I didn't know when, but someday I was going to pay him back for that. "He didn't do jack-shit to you today—not compared to what he could do. You dig?"

I said, "Do you know a man named Pennyfeather?"

Johnny and Eugene glanced at each other.

"You really want a good one, don't you?" Johnny said.

"Then I take it you do know Pennyfeather?"

"Pops," Johnny said, and in a curious way he spoke out of pity and not anger, "I can really be a bad guy. Now why don't you go get in your car and get out of here?" He nodded to my arm, which I was still rubbing. "I'm sorry if I overdid it. I've just got this temper, all right?"

In the window now I saw the four-year-old girl, wearing dirty pink pajamas, pressing her sweet dirty face against the pane, watching me.

I said, "Why don't you tell the police everything you know? They're going to be here sooner or later."

"Just get out of here, pal, and that's my last warning."

"He's getting pissed again," Eugene said. "Usually he isn't this nice."

I sighed, rubbed my hand again, and started off the porch.

The little girl watched me as I started down the stairs. She looked sadder than any child her age ever should.

20

Before checking out the second address in Conroy's log, I went to Donutland and had two cups of coffee and a donut. The sweet-faced waitress kept looking at my hands and how they still shook. It's nice to tell yourself that in your prime you could have handled punks like the two at Kathy Stacek's place, but the fact was that I'd never been especially tough. When I lost my temper I was liable to pick up something and hit you with it, but I'd never been gifted with quick or terrible fists. Even back in my detective days, I'd always fought only as a last resort. So now I shook from lost pride and animal fear and great useless rage.

I sat for a while looking around at the other people in the small shop on Mt. Vernon Road. They talked in little groups or sat staring off alone just as I did. This was one of winter's first overcast days and it was taking its toll.

The second address was a new Drive-Mart farther out Mt. Vernon Road. There were six pumps on the drive and an overhang to protect customers from the worst of the elements. Inside, the mini-grocery store had the air of a long-ago corner store. There would be everything from baby food to cigarettes to toilet paper; the only thing there wouldn't be was an immigrant Irish or Jewish owner, the way Costello's or Mendlebaum's used to.

"You know what used to be here?" I asked the girl behind the counter.

"A lot."

"A lot?"

"Vacant lot. I know because I used to live in this neighborhood and I always played baseball with my brothers here."

"Oh."

She grinned. She had bright blue eyes and soft bottle blonde hair and that peculiar vulnerability that accrues to young girls with dental braces. "It's weird when you think about it."

"What's weird?"

"Oh, you know, you play baseball on this vacant lot when you're growing up and then you move away and then fourteen years later you move back and work in a store that's built on the same vacant lot. It's just kind of weird, you know, how things happen over the years."

I smiled. "That's pretty smart, what you just said."

"Aw."

"Really." I gave her a small wave and walked out.

There was a pay phone on the corner. I walked over to it, a hard winter wind pushing me faster.

I phoned a friend of mine named Sweeney.

"Can you hold on?"

"Sure."

"It may take a little while."

"That's fine."

Whenever I need to find out something about real estate, I call Sweeney. He works in the courthouse. He's about my age and he's a Democrat the way other people are Hare Krishnas. FDR was the Father, JFK the Son, and Jimmy Carter the Holy Ghost. The first two I might be able to buy, but

Carter I never could stand. Maybe it was that psychotic smile.

Usually, Sweeney can find the previous owner of a given address in under five minutes.

This time, it took him eight. "Marvin Scribbins. Owned it for fifteen years. 1971–1986."

"He sold it?"

"Ummm. To a developer who put up some kind of Dairy Queen deal. Insty-Freeze. Lead balloon."

"Huh?"

"Lead balloon. You know, 'sank like a lead balloon.' "

"Oh, yeah."

"Then they sold it to the corporation that owns the Drive-Marts."

"Anything on Marvin Scribbins?"

He riffled some papers. "Just the usual stuff. No forwarding, if that's what you're looking for."

"So he could still be here in Cedar Rapids?"

"I suppose."

"Well, I'll check it out. Thanks."

He said, "I didn't see you at the Jefferson-Jackson Day dinner this year."

"Busy, I guess."

"The party really needs your help, Walsh. It needs everybody's help."

"I'm going to pitch in. I promise."

He laughed. "I don't know why I put up with this stuff."

"You know something? Neither do I."

He laughed again and hung up.

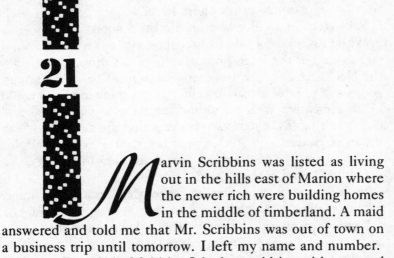

21

Marvin Scribbins was listed as living out in the hills east of Marion where the newer rich were building homes in the middle of timberland. A maid answered and told me that Mr. Scribbins was out of town on a business trip until tomorrow. I left my name and number.

In the East Side Maidrite I had a maidrite with mustard and pickles and a bottle of Hamms, the mid-afternoon meal I started eating in my fifties, one of the ways I keep my energy up. Finished, I smoked two cigarettes, one-third of my daily allotment. They tasted better than they had any right to.

In the car again, snow beginning to splatter on the windshield, I drove down First Avenue past the crumbling houses that only thirty years ago had been the special province of the upper middle class, down past Coe College and the refurbished buildings that looked sleek and formidable even in the afternoon gloom, and on down to the beginnings of the business district.

Paul Heckart's building was a prim three-story brick that had recently been sandblasted. With its tinted and sealed windows, it appeared almost brand new. Inside, everything *was* brand new—bright wallcoverings, carpeting, doors, even the office furnishings. The effect of all this was apparently good on the workers. Everybody moved around quickly, desk to desk, floor to floor, and when they spoke to one another it was with the kind of pleasantness that can't be faked. There was a good working atmosphere here.

Paul Heckart's office was on the third floor.

While I waited for him in a reception area, I walked around and looked at the large photographs of the office furnishings the Heckart Company designed and built. The stuff was gorgeous and not quite real. You just didn't think anybody could be that creative with something as mundane as desks and chairs and tables, even wastebaskets that did not in any way resemble wastebaskets. No wonder Paul Heckart and his brother were two of the most successful men in the city.

"Hello," Paul Heckart said.

In the daylight, he appeared bigger than he had last night, a long-striding man who was probably most at home on the golf course, tanned, white-haired, firm-jawed, and with a grip that shamed mine. Adjusting his regimental-striped tie inside his three-piece blue suit, he said, seeming worried, "Has something happened, Mr. Walsh?"

"Not that I know of. I just wondered if I could talk to you."

"Of course," he said. "Of course you can."

To the fetching young receptionist with the Katharine Hepburn auburn hair and the wry Myrna Loy gaze, he said, "Trish, we'll be in my conference room."

"Should I interrupt?"

"Not unless it's really an emergency."

She nodded, and he led me down a hall that was just as sumptuous as the rest of the layout.

The conference room was very conservative: mahogany furnishings and wall trimmings with dark blue carpeting that made you feel, at first, as if you were walking into quicksand. From the large window in the east wall you could see all of downtown, the Teleconnect building looming especially large only a few blocks away.

He poured us each a cup of coffee from a silver server that

probably cost half as much as my car. When we were seated across the conference table from each other, he said, "Now, how may I help you, Mr. Walsh?"

"I thought that maybe you could tell me a few things about the Pennyfeather family. I can't quite bring them into focus."

"I'm not sure what you mean." He looked, for the first time, vaguely uncomfortable. Before I could explain further, he said, "Before we start, there's something I'd better tell you."

"All right."

"I'm the closest friend they've got, and in turn they're my closest friends. The entire family. I'm sorry if I looked a little apprehensive there—when you asked me to talk about them—but I just couldn't bring myself to say anything negative about them."

"I'm not asking for anything negative, Mr. Heckart. I'm just trying to find out what happened twelve years ago so I can learn something more about last night."

"You think they're connected?"

"Possibly; probably."

"What would you like me to tell you?"

"About the family relationship, for one thing. I don't think I've ever seen a family that close-knit before."

He smiled. "They're like a TV family, aren't they?"

"Do they spend as much time together as they seem to?"

"Yes, unfortunately, they do, and I'm afraid that's why neither David nor Carolyn is married any longer. Their respective spouses just couldn't handle that kind of closeness."

"Oh?"

"Have you ever been around a family whose only reality is themselves?"

I shrugged. "I suppose; I guess I'm not sure."

"Well, no matter how often or cordially they try to include you, you can easily develop the sense that because you're not a blood part of them somehow you just don't belong. Again, this isn't anything the family does consciously. But as an out-sider, you certainly could get that impression."

"Were the Pennyfeathers like this even before George went away to prison?"

"Oh, my, yes. They've always been like that. First George and Lisa and then the kids." He shook his Roman senator head. "That's what was so ludicrous about the charge that Karl Jankov and Lisa Pennyfeather were having an affair. She was so completely wrapped up in her family that it just never could have happened."

" 'Never' is a pretty strong word."

"But in this case it's the appropriate word."

"So you don't think that George killed Jankov?"

"No offense, Mr. Walsh, I know you were the detective in charge of the case, and I know that with that Stacek girl's testimony the obvious suspect was George—but he didn't do it. I'm sure of it."

I sipped some coffee. It was very good. "Could we talk about him? Jankov?"

"Of course. If you'd like."

"During the trial, I got the impression he'd been your right-hand man, that anything that needed doing in the company, he'd do for you."

"That's a fair impression, I suppose."

"Did you like him as a person?"

"To be honest, no."

"Why not?"

"With Karl you always saw all the gears working. He never did anything that didn't advance his career or put himself in a good light. He was like this little animal that needed constant attention and reward. As valuable as he was, his toadying made me uncomfortable."

"But he was an effective vice president for you?"

"Very. We enjoyed a great period of growth during his tenure here."

"Did he ever make a pass at Lisa Pennyfeather?"

"Probably." He laughed. "For Karl there were two kinds of rewards. A pat on the head from the boss and the approval of women who came from a higher social class than he had. Karl was a poor boy who'd been gifted with great cunning and energy—if not exactly brains—and very good looks. He appealed especially to women who wanted some excitement in their lives." He poured us more coffee. "On any given day, that would describe about half the women at the country club. That was Karl's 'circuit,' if you will." He chuckled. "He did a lot of 'recruiting' out there."

"Do you think it could have been one of those women who killed him?"

"No, I don't, Mr. Walsh. I know who killed him."

The certainty in his voice surprised me. "You do?"

"Of course. His wife, Terri."

"Why would she kill him?"

"Terri was—and still is, I'd assume—very much like Karl. Graced with cunning and energy, and very much upwardly mobile. She came from the same kind of background. Terri had one problem that Karl didn't, however."

"What's that?"

"Jealousy. In those days, anyway, she was pathologically jealous. If she hadn't disrupted the work day so much around here, I might even have felt sorry for her."

"She made scenes?"

"Scenes?" He made a sour face. "Try slapping Karl right in his office with a client present. Or interrupting him with phone calls during key presentations. Or waiting out in his car for him with a revolver she fired into the roof. The county attorney could have brought this out at the trial, but he was interested only in George. George made for bigger headlines."

Just then there was a discreet knock on the door. I was assuming it would be the receptionist. Instead, it was Heckart's brother, Richard. He came in without saying anything.

He wore a brown suit cut a little more fashionably than Paul's, and black horn-rims that lent him the air of a man intellectually intent. As he came over to me, he said to his brother, "When you get a chance, go down to the lab and look at my design for the new desk. I think I really hit it this time."

Paul laughed. "You remember my brother, Richard, Mr. Walsh. He was just trying to tell you in his subtle way that he's really the brains of our company. He does all the major design work. All I am is a glorified peddler."

Without being asked, Richard sat down and poured himself some coffee. "I heard you were up here, Mr. Walsh. I thought I'd just come up and say hello."

Heard I was up here? Who had told him? And why?

"My brother likes to know everything that's going on," Paul Heckart laughed. "It's from his army days. He was a colonel, and he never got over his taste for being in command—even though technically, I'm older and the one that my father left in command." An uneasy melancholy filled his gaze. "Dad died while Richard was in Korea. He went very slowly." He offered me a social smile. "It's funny, I can always get that way about Dad."

Richard Heckart said, "You're confusing Mr. Walsh here, Paul. He probably thinks we don't get along. And we do."

"Just as long as I do everything you tell me to, little brother," Paul Heckart said. He spoke with cold authority. There was nothing ironic in his voice. He was quite serious.

"Your brother was just telling me about Jankov," I said, uncomfortable with the tension between them.

"Ah, Mr. Jankov," Richard Heckart said. He shook his head with quick and pointed disgust. "I never cared for him. I can't even say I'm sorry that he was murdered." He stared at me. "I keep forgetting that you're the detective who arrested poor George."

I nodded.

"It's damned funny how these things turn out," he said, rueful as always. Last night I'd had the impression that he might be less skilled socially than his brother. What I'd missed was the fact that they simply represented two different styles—the senatorial gloss of his brother, his own barely disguised contempt for most subjects and most people. He'd probably made a fine colonel. "Your representing George now, I mean."

"I'm just trying to help out a little."

"And of course you wouldn't think of taking any money for it."

"Richard, for Christ's sake," Paul Heckart said.

"I'm not sure it's a good idea any of us talk to you, Mr. Walsh. Frankly, given your ties to the local *gendarmes*, I wouldn't be surprised if you told them everything you found out." Richard Heckart smiled as he spoke. "I wouldn't think that at all unfair of you, either, as far as that goes. A man who was a detective as long as you—naturally your first loyalty is to the force."

"It wasn't the 'force,' Mr. Heckart. I was with the Linn County Sheriff's Department."

"Whatever. You know what I'm talking about."

Flushing now, his right hand curved into an impressive fist, Paul Heckart said, "You seem to be forgetting something, brother."

"And what would that be, brother?"

"That Mr. Walsh came to see me. And that what the two of us talk about is none of your goddamn business."

Ironically, the tension eased after Paul Heckart swore. The animosity was plain and open now, and it was always better this way than hiding behind masks and bitchiness.

"You'd like me to leave?" Richard said. There was a tartness to him that was neither appealing nor amusing.

"Please," Paul said, "so we may finish our conversation."

Richard was on his feet now. He looked at me. He smiled again. "Would you like me to tell you what Paul will tell you about me as soon as I leave the room?"

Now, I was the one with red in my cheeks. I dropped my gaze. My palms were gummy with sweat. This was like having Sister Mary Frances make me stand in front of the fourth-grade class that time and apologize for writing the word "shit" on the blackboard.

"He will say," Richard Heckart went on, "that I'm just overprotective of both him and the company, that I'm as reclusive as the Pennyfeathers, and that the reason I hated Jankov was quite simple—he had an affair with my wife. It took me a long time to get over it. A long time. It wasn't good for my wife, me, or our children. We spent thousands of dollars seeing a marriage counselor before we had any kind of home life again."

"None of this came out during the trial," I said.

Paul Heckart said, "For just the reason I hear in your voice—because if it had, Richard would have been a prime suspect. And I knew for certain that Richard had had nothing to do with Jankov's murder."

"How could you know that?" I asked.

"Because during the established time of death, Richard was with me out on my boat. It was just a small craft, one I generally keep moored out at Ellis. I use it sometimes for fishing trips. We went to a lake home owned by a friend named Delaney. Usually, we would have gone to our own cabin, but I'd given that to the Pennyfeathers."

"I see."

Richard said, "The cabin's been in the family for three generations, Mr. Walsh." He looked directly at his brother. "We've all taken guests up there. Paul used to take George fishing, and sometimes he'd take young David for a weekend every once in a while. Is there something about the cabin that interests you?"

Something had changed his attitude. He was no longer bitchy; he wanted to understand my curiosity, and that meant good behavior.

"I just thought it might look awfully convenient to a county attorney—a prime suspect with such a good alibi. A respected brother and a cabin in the woods."

"Meaning what, Mr. Walsh?" Richard asked.

I decided to rattle him some. "Meaning that it might have looked contrived. Your alibi. To anybody of a suspicious nature."

"And is that your nature, Mr. Walsh? Suspicious?"

"I suppose."

"Well, whether you believe it or not—and I don't give a damn if you do—I was with Paul that whole evening."

"That's true, Mr. Walsh," Paul said.

"I wasn't making any accusations," I said to Richard Heckart. "I was only making a comment."

"I'll accept it at that, then." He surprised me by putting out his hand. He had the steely family grip. "I'm sorry if this got nasty. I'm naturally upset over what's happened with poor George. You can understand that."

"Of course," I said, and in fact I supposed I could.

Richard Heckart nodded goodbye to his brother and left. He closed the door quietly.

"Well," Paul Heckart said, "I don't know about you, but that isn't something I'd care to go through again."

I laughed. "I've been through a lot worse."

He frowned. "He's just very afraid we'll let Dad down."

"How would you do that?"

"By letting something get beyond our control. That's the military man in Richard. He wants to control everything. He always looked at this mess with Jankov as something that could ultimately hurt the company. That's why he gets so angry about it, though he'd never admit it. We were raised to believe that the business our great-grandfather started several gen-

erations ago was something to be kept in impeccable condition—like a shrine of some sort. I'm afraid Richard got a little
too much of that instilled in him. He tends to get feisty and
arrogant any time he perceives the company is threatened."

"You really were with him the night of Jankov's murder?"

"You think he's lying to you, Mr. Walsh?"

"That isn't exactly an answer."

"Well, here *is* an exact answer, Mr. Walsh. Yes, my brother
was with me all the time that night."

"Fine. I'll accept that then."

He laughed. "Now we're getting into it, aren't we?"

"Nothing major, Mr. Heckart. You've been very helpful,
and I appreciate it."

"I just hope you or the police can find the person who killed
that poor woman last night. Have the authorities learned much
about her yet?"

"Not much."

"In the gazebo. It seems such a waste."

"It generally is, Mr. Heckart. Murder."

I tugged up the collar of my car coat. I put out my hand.
We shook. I walked to the door.

"If you think of anything about the Jankov case that you
think is useful, please call me."

"Why don't you try Terri Jankov? As I told you, she would
be my first suspect."

"Maybe I will. Well, thanks again."

At the door, he said, "Please don't judge either my brother
or me on our little disagreement this afternoon."

"I won't."

"We're just concerned for George."

"Of course."

"But I really would look up Terri. She tried to kill him a
few times before somebody actually did kill him."

"Something else that didn't come out at the trial."

"I'm not sure anybody took her attempts very seriously.

Sometimes murder attempts—especially between lovers—are like suicide attempts. Really just calling out for attention."

"I suppose."

"I hope you'll look her up."

I smiled. "After all you've told me about her, I guess I don't have much choice, do I?"

22

On the other side of the door you could hear Barry Manilow complaining about how various people had done him wrong and he was getting tired of it. That was a modest joke between Faith and me, anyway—she says that Tony Bennett (who I like) always sounds drunk, and I say that Manilow (who she likes) is always complaining. About the only singer we like in common is Elvis Presley. When you had two teenagers, you learned to like Elvis. You didn't have much choice.

When she opened my door, she put a *shush*ing finger to her lips. "Hoyt's asleep."

I nodded and went in and noticed immediately how hard she'd been working all day. Everything had been dusted, set right, picked up, polished. The place looked great.

There was even a frilly white apron tied around her lovely hips. She'd once told me she considered aprons the ultimate symbol of a woman's subjugation. She must have changed her mind.

She came up and kissed me gently on the lips and said, in a half-whisper, "Do you suppose we could make love? I mean, is this the right time to ask you?"

I smiled. "I guess we could find out."

"Could I ask you something, though?"

"Sure."

"Don't touch my breasts. I think I'll just leave this blouse on if you don't mind."

"Fine, hon. Fine."

There are a lot of different reasons to make love and lust is generally the least of them. When I was in Italy in the final months of the war, I slept once a day with an Italian woman because I was convinced these would be my last hours and I needed to do something human and profound. I made love out of fear—fear that nothing made any sense and that I had to make some small connection between myself and another person before I faced oblivion. When Sharon was dying, I made love to comfort her. She was facing oblivion, too, and though her religious faith was greater than mine, I saw in the nooks and crannies of her final days the fear of extinction that comes to all animals, probably even those of the lower orders if we only knew how to understand them properly. When I met Faith, I made love to heal myself. The first time we went to bed I could scarcely get an erection. There had been too much loneliness and loss in my life for anything as positive as desire. But gradually it happened and soon enough I heard myself laughing as we tumbled into bed one night, and things were fine ever after. Faith had no idea what she'd given me; no idea. And now it was my turn to repay her.

In the gray dusk, the smell of roast beef cooking in red wine filling the apartment, we made slow gentle love on the couch, with the sound off and Bullwinkle making broad pantomime gestures to Rocket J. Squirrel, and Hoyt snoring sleep from his tiny pink mouth in the bedroom.

Several times my hand went instinctively to her breast, then at the last minute drew back.

Afterward there were none of the frail, insecure questions lovers usually ask to be reassured that they have given pleasure to their mates. We were way beyond ego; way beyond.

She lay on top of me, her head on my chest. When she spoke, she raised her small head a bit and spoke off to the side, as if addressing a ghostly presence.

"I'm sorry about not letting you touch my breasts."

"I understand, Faith. Hell."

Silence. Her head back down.

I said, "We're going to be celebrating tomorrow. You'll see. After the mammogram."

Silence.

I stroked her fine soft hair. When she started to cry, shaking there on my body like a sad little girl, I held her tight as I thought wise, and said nothing.

Late afternoon became full night, headlights playing off the north wall as cars sped out the avenue swishing through the wet snow, and you could hear in the silence a TV set in one apartment, laughter in another, an old man's lonely curse in yet another.

"Why don't we go lie down with Hoyt?" she said.

We stood up, dressed; I went into the bedroom while she headed for the bathroom. I lay next to Hoyt, giving him one finger to grasp while he slept. You could hear her peeing and then the toilet flushing and then the basin water running. She came in and lay on the other side of Hoyt, the bedsprings squeaking slightly. It was darker in this room. When head-lights came they played against the window wet with snow, the melting liquid briefly the color of gold in the splash of lights. From the closet came the faint odor of mothballs; from the bureau the faint scent of Old Spice. Hoyt let out with a considerable fart. We were desperate for something to laugh about and this was it. She reached over Hoyt's head and took my hand. She was asleep in a few minutes.

After we woke up, we went into the kitchen. She set dinner on the table.

"You want me to go with you?" I asked.

"I go back and forth."

"I'd be happy to."

"I thought you were working for the Pennyfeathers."

"I am. But I'd take time off."

"How's it going?"

"I'm not sure."

"You still think Pennyfeather killed that man?"

"Yes."

"You think he killed the woman last night?"

"I'm not sure."

She sighed, put her head down. She'd gone to the trouble of a candlelight dinner, and now she wasn't eating.

"You going to get Marcia to babysit?"

"Ummm. If she can, anyway. Guess I'd better talk to her before she goes out to Rockwell tonight." She paused. "Why would he kill her?"

"Pennyfeather?"

"Ummm."

"I'm not sure. You really interested in it?"

"I don't want to talk about—my situation anymore. I'm sick of it. That's the trouble with being sick—it makes you the focus of everything, and you get tired of your ego long before you get tired of the illness. You know?"

"Yeah."

"So what happens if Pennyfeather didn't kill that man?"

"His name was Jankov and I'm not sure what happens if Pennyfeather turns up innocent."

"It's a possibility?"

"I suppose."

"Do you have any other suspects?"

"Not really, though there are several people who seem to have some peculiar bearing on the case."

"Such as?"

The phone rang. Immediately Hoyt began crying. She got up and went into the bedroom. I went into the kitchen to the wall phone. "Hello."

"Is this Mr. Walsh?"

"Yes."

"Hi. This is Dolores."

The name and voice sounded familiar but I couldn't quite place them.

"This morning. Out in front of Stella Czmek's place."

"Oh. Right. Dolores. How are you?"

"I'm fine. But I'm not sure Bainbridge is."

"No?"

"No."

"What's wrong?"

"I was walkin' to the store and I saw somebody go in there. Then when I was walkin' back I heard somebody scream. I'm sure it was Bainbridge."

"You're at home now?"

"Yeah."

"Can you see Bainbridge's house from where you are?"

"No. But I can go out on the porch."

"All right. You know what kind of car his visitor was driving?"

"Some kind of green car."

I thought of Conroy, the private investigator. "Could it be a Chevrolet?"

"Could be. They kind of all look alike these days."

"You'll go check?"

"Be right back."

Faith came carrying Hoyt. She brought him over and leaned him into me. He gave me a small warm wet kiss on my cheek.

Dolores came back. "Car's gone. No lights on in Bainbridge's. You comin' over?"

"Thought I might, yes."

"See you in a little bit, then."

"Thanks, Dolores. Thanks very much."

I had just turned to hang up the phone when Faith said, "I won't mind."

"You won't?"

"No, I like to see you working. You seem more—complete, I guess."

"I suppose you're right. But—"

"I'll be fine. Really."

I leaned over to Hoyt and chucked him under the chin. "You take good care of her, you hear?"

He gave me a small solid punch on my forehead.

"I could be back late."

"That's all right. I'll probably pick up a little and watch some movie on TV and doze off."

"There's a movie called *The Gunfighter* on cable."

"A western?"

"Yeah. Oh, I forgot."

"I'm sure they're good. I just don't appreciate them, I guess."

"This one's a little different." Then I thought of how he dies in the end. "But I don't think you'll like it." I went over and picked up the *TV Guide*. "You're in luck."

"What?"

"They're showing one of those colorized deals of *Casablanca* tonight."

"I love *Casablanca*."

"That's what I figured," I said.

I kissed her, I kissed Hoyt, and I left.

23

By the time I reached Ellis Boulevard the snow was coming down in earnest, cars spinning back wheels at stoplights and sliding forward in little unwanted bursts of power, people leaning over windshields and scooping off handfuls of cold numbing white stuff after having forgotten to buy gloves and scrapers, tiny old people walking with sad comic caution down slippery sidewalks.

There were no lights in Mr. Bainbridge's.

I was on the sidewalk about ten seconds when Dolores appeared, bundled up in a large red coat. She grinned. "My kids still don't think you're really a private detective."

I smiled. "Did you get a look at the man in the car?"

"Not really."

"About how long ago do you think he left?"

"Twenty, twenty-five minutes."

"And you haven't seen Bainbridge on the street?"

"No."

"Maybe he just went to sleep."

"Not Bainbridge. He always watchin' that religious channel on the TV and keeps the sound up real loud, especially when they playin' music. Man, does he like loud music."

"Why don't I go up to the door?"

"Go ahead, but it won't get you nothin'."

"There's a positive attitude."

Her laughing behind me, I went up to the door. Through the small glass of the door window, I looked inside. Nothing. No light; no sign of life. I knocked. It was like tossing a coin down a very deep well. It got lost before it touched bottom.

"Tol' ya," Dolores said.

I turned around. "I appreciate all the confidence you have in me."

"You sure are a smart-ass."

I turned back to the door and knocked again. Two cars of teenagers went by. Several generations of Cedar Rapids kids had driven down Ellis Boulevard, all in search of the same elusive things. Pretty soon they'd have beer bellies and mean factory foremen and then it would be their own kids who went looking for all those lovely things young people make fools of themselves over. You could hear their radios now; you could smell their underage beers.

"You scared to try the side door?" Dolores said.

"You'd be great during a burglary. You could stand down on the sidewalk and shout out instructions to me."

She started laughing again.

So of course I went around the side of the house, sticking to the smashed concrete walkway, sort of bobbing up and down for a dark useless look inside the side windows.

I pounded on the side door with the authority of a cop effecting a bust. And got, for my trouble, the same response I'd gotten from the front door.

Dolores came around to the side of the house. "You want inside?"

"I don't have a key."

"The way I've got in mind, you won't need a key."

"Really?"

"Really, Mr. Private Eye."

"Why're you being so helpful?"

"Because this will make a great story at my Amway party next week."

"I see."

"I hope you find him dead."

"Bainbridge?"

"You got it. First, 'cause I'd like to see him dead, the way he feels about black people. Second, 'cause it would make my story better."

"Well, I sure hope I can oblige you, Dolores, and find a corpse inside."

"You ever actually find one before?" Now she didn't seem quite so certain she wanted me to find Bainbridge dead.

"Couple of times, when I was with the Sheriff's Department."

"It scare you?"

"Didn't scare me but I've never forgotten them. One was a two-year-old that the mother had walked off and left. He died when the gas started leaking."

"You believe in the death penalty?"

"Yep."

"So do I, for shit like that any way. How about the other one?"

"Old man who'd fallen down and hit his head on the edge of the coffee table. The fall induced a stroke. It was two weeks before they found him."

"Musta stunk."

"You wouldn't have believed it."

She said, "I shouldn't a said that."

"Said what?"

"About Bainbridge."

"Oh."

"I don't really wish he was dead."

"I know."

"It's just how he carries on about black people."

"I understand. I really do."

"So maybe we better check him out. For his own sake."

"Good idea."

"Let me lead you around back."

She got ahead of me on the walk in her big red coat. The darkness took some of the color from the material. But nothing could take the confidence from her stride.

In the rear were two slanting doors leading to a cellar. I hadn't seen one of these in thirty years. She went over and opened one of the doors. It made a *scraw*ing, rusty-hinged sound as she pulled it back. She said, "This is as far as I go. I got to get back home. One of my kids is sick."

"I certainly appreciate this."

"I really shouldn't a said that about him."

"It's nice to know you're guilty about it."

"You bein' a smart-ass again?"

"No; knowing you're feeling guilty means you didn't really mean it in the first place."

She laughed. "You're a strange man, Walsh. Just like my husband."

"Thanks for helping." I put my hand out and we shook. She waved goodbye and said, "I'll be going down the alley here," and then she was gone.

Up from the cellar came the dank smells of mildew and dampness. The place appeared to be deep as a pit.

I put a tentative foot through the slanting doorway. I half-expected a monster to grab it and eat it.

My foot found a step; my other foot found another step. I started my descent, using my Zippo, best as I could, as a frail torch here in the gloom.

The mildew smell got overpowering. The dampness at once seeped through my clothes and began brushing at my flesh like something wraithlike and unclean.

The wooden stairs were warped. Twice I nearly tripped and fell forward. Quickly enough, my Zippo went out.

By the time I reached the floor of the cellar, darkness had sealed me inside. Behind me the open cellar door showed only the faintest evidence of night sky. It was as if somebody had closed the door.

Ahead of me I heard the *whoof* of a furnace catching wind. Keeping my hand ahead of me like an antenna, I moved down a dirt floor path between cardboard boxes that had been piled high on either side. Around a corner, I saw the blue glow of a gas jet. I walked over to the furnace, feeling as exultant as the prehistoric man who had discovered fire.

From the plump belly of the furnace came warmth and enough light to see the outline of rickety wooden stairs rising at an angle to the upstairs of the house.

I went up the stairs carefully, afraid they would literally disintegrate beneath me. The wooden steps were rank with the smell of mildew. The rot had seeped into the deepest fiber of the wood.

At the top I found a door and tried the knob. Unlocked. I put my head against the door and listened, hearing nothing but the groaning noises old houses make.

I opened the door and went inside.

During my time as a detective, I had seen many houses where lonely old people had died. Invariably, I'd found at least some evidence of the pack-rat mentality. I'm not sure what it's all about. Perhaps it's as simple as this—amassing things is a way of building a fortress against the outside world, a variation on the idea that some fat people have that their fatness forms a protective wall around them, inside of which they are secure. Whatever the impulse, a surprising number of the elderly follow up on it. You find houses and apartments packed with newspapers, canned goods, a jungle of ancient furniture, clothes, anything that a human being can bring inside.

Bainbridge's house was not much different except for one

thing: The rows and rows of packing crates that filled each room were far more orderly than you usually encountered. In fact, my first impression was that the place was a warehouse of sorts. After looking through my third room on the first floor, that was still my impression.

Enough dirty electric light came through the windows to guide me through the first floor. I saw all the things I'd expected to find—lumpy, dumpy furnishings; wallspace packed with paintings of Christ, the sort that depict him as Elvis Presley's religious older brother; the smells of cigarettes and cold pizza boxes and cough medicine and liniment for tired bones; and a glowing TV set in a small room that looked like one of those forlorn little nooks you see in VA hospitals, where you spend half an hour with the carnage of a man hacking his way through the final stages of lung cancer. An empty Pepsi bottle lay overturned on a coffee table that had only three legs, like a maimed dog, and several ashtrays with gnarled butts.

On the tube a TV minister was bowing his head to pray for people. I hoped he was including me. I couldn't be sure because the sound was off.

The only thing I knew for sure was that Bainbridge wasn't on the first floor. I had even checked all the closets.

Above me stretched a staircase that rose toward and then vanished into utter darkness. I tried the light switch. Nothing; no light on the staircase. I listened for the reassuring sounds of traffic on Ellis. I started up the stairs. Long ago they had been carpeted; now the carpeting was barely a nub, and the stairs made more noise than an old man with asthma. Decades-old dust filled my nose and mouth; I coughed.

I was two steps across the landing at the top of the stairs when I stumbled over something. It might have been one of those comic pratfalls we all take from time to time, arms flailing, mouth yawped open without any dignity whatsoever, head aimed directly for the floor. But this was different because as I started to fall, my foot kicked into something that I recognized immediately as a human body.

I didn't have much doubt about who it belonged to.

I landed on all fours, which saved me a headache anyway. I crawled over to Bainbridge and tried to see him, but it was too dark. I stood up and started groping around for a light switch. I found one in the bathroom, the smell of which was acrid. I soon enough discovered why. Either Bainbridge didn't believe in flushing or the toilet didn't work properly. Cupping a hand over my nose to kill the smell, I wobbled back to Bainbridge.

On his forehead you could see a faint red identation where somebody had hit him, probably with a fist. At his age, in his condition, it hadn't taken much to knock him out.

I went into the bathroom, cupping my nose again, and soaked one towel in cold water, grabbed another that was dry, and started back to him. Then I stopped. Though the bathroom was small, it was packed tight with the same kind of crates that filled the first floor. Here, in the light, I saw that the crates had a company name printed on them: Vandersee Import-Export.

I thought of Stella Czmek and how her fortunes had improved so abruptly and mysteriously once she'd gone to work for Vandersee. Then I remembered that Vandersee had died a few years ago. Now I was curious about how he'd died.

Bainbridge had started to moan by the time I knelt next to him again and began to daub his face with cold water.

"Bainbridge?"

Moaning.

"Bainbridge? Who hit you?"

Moaning.

"Bainbridge. I want to help you. Tell me what happened here tonight."

Still moaning, but now the tiny mad eyes beginning to open and peer up at me; the eyes of a predatory bird.

"Bainbridge. Was it Conroy who was here tonight? A private detective named Conroy?"

He spoke then, and for all his pictures of Jesus, for all his Biblical talk of sin and salvation, his words were most inappropriate. He said, "You go to hell."

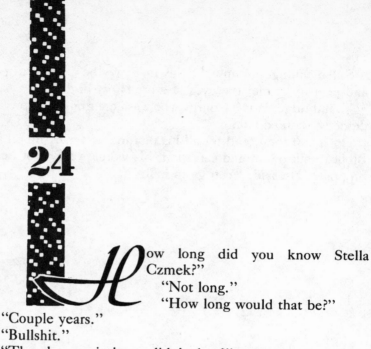

24

"How long did you know Stella Czmek?"

"Not long."

"How long would that be?"

"Couple years."

"Bullshit."

"They let you in here, didn't they?"

" 'They'?"

"Those nigger women."

"I'm asking you about Stella Czmek."

"I don't know anything about her."

"That's why you've got a houseful of crates from Vandersee's."

"She just stored the stuff here. Gave me money for it."

"What's in the boxes?"

"Don't know. Never looked."

"You really expect me to believe that?"

"I don't have to answer your questions."

I decided to roll the dice. "Why don't you call the police?"

"What?"

"You heard me. Call the police."

"I'll call them when I feel like it."

"You're afraid to call them."

"That's a lie."

"Because of what's in those boxes, that's why."

"You leave them boxes alone."

We sat in his bedroom upstairs. I had stretched him out on the bed and put the wet towel across his forehead. I sat on a straight-back chair across the room. He stared at the ceiling. Above him was another painting of Jesus, a velvet painting. In this one Jesus appeared to be scowling. I could understand why.

In the street below traffic *shoosh*ed along the damp boulevard. Somewhere nearby a dog barked. Bainbridge's breathing was very loud. He didn't sound so good.

I had a cigarette going. My lungs probably didn't sound so good, either. I said, "Who was here tonight?"

"Nobody."

"You knocked yourself out?"

"I tripped."

"Right. Was it Conroy?"

The way he blinked, I could tell he knew who I was talking about. "I don't know no Conroy."

"He drives a new green Chevrolet. It was seen parked along the side street about an hour ago."

"Those nigger women again."

"What does Conroy want from you?"

"Nothing."

"Why did he come here?"

"He didn't come here."

"What's in the boxes?"

"Vases."

"Anything else?"

"Just vases."

"From where?"

"Hong Kong."

"Why would she want all those vases stored here?"

"You'd have to ask her."

"You just stay on the bed."

"Where you going?"

"Going to start looking through the boxes."

"Bullshit."

"You've got some mouth for a reverend."

"You leave them boxes alone."

He started to get up. I pushed him down harder than I needed to. He cracked his head on the metal bedpost. He said another word reverends aren't supposed to say.

I said, "Why don't you call the police?"

"You leave me alone."

"Why not, Bainbridge? Why not call the police?"

"You bastard. I'm an old man."

"In case you hadn't noticed, so am I."

"Who the hell you work for, anyway?"

I pointed to the bed. "You stay there. You hear me?"

Twenty minutes later I'd gone through ten of the packing crates on the second floor. Vases were what he'd promised, and vases were what I found. Vases. Cheap blue ones and cheap purple ones and cheap yellow ones, each with raised dragon figures, each with a somewhat lopsided mouth in which to put cut flowers.

For my trouble I had received a bruised thumb, having never been much good with a hammer, a body slick with sweat, and the growing suspicion that my suspicions were unfounded. Maybe Stella Czmek had taken on Vandersee inventory as a favor to Vandersee, or with an eye to setting up her own import-export business. Or just because she plain liked vases.

Whatever, there seemed to be no sinister intent in storing them here.

I changed my mind as soon as I found the open crate on the bottom of a pile. The first thing I checked for was some small difference between it and the other boxes and I found it without much trouble at all, a small rubber-stamp black star along the bottom of the crate. The second thing I checked on was the inside of the box, which was where I found two more eyesore purple vases, and an indentation in the bottom of the box where some sort of book had lain. At least I assumed it had been a book. That's what it looked like under the dull glow of the flashlight I'd borrowed from Bainbridge's bathroom.

I spent the next twenty minutes checking all the other boxes, upstairs and downstairs, for sight of the black star again. It was not to be found.

I took the empty box back to Bainbridge's bedroom.

He lay propped up against the back of the bed now. He had his Bible spread out on his lap. From somewhere he'd produced a pair of ancient wire-rim glasses. He probably played Scrooge in the local KKK chapter's version of "A Christmas Carol."

"What does this black star mean?"

"Wouldn't know."

"Look at it."

"Don't need to look at it. Don't know what it means."

"Look at it."

He sighed and swung his head around. You could still see where he'd been smacked hard in the forehead. He looked enfeebled. I wished I could feel sorry for him but I couldn't."

"Don't have no idea what it is."

"This is what Conroy wanted, isn't it? He's the one who opened this box tonight, isn't he?"

"Don't know no Conroy."

"What was in the book?"

"What book?"

"There's an indentation on the bottom of the box. That means that when this was shipped from Hong Kong, somebody hid some sort of contraband in the bottom of the box."

He went back to his Bible. "Wouldn't know about anything like that."

I grabbed him by the shirt and yanked him around. I slapped him once hard across the mouth.

His Bible dropped on the floor. He put his face down on the bed and started sobbing. He sounded sick and crazy.

"What the hell's going on here, Bainbridge, and what does Conroy have to do with this?"

He waved me off, apparently afraid I was going to hurt him some more.

I went over and sat in the straight-back chair and lighted a cigarette and stared down at the boulevard and the traffic lost behind the white wavering sheet of snow. The smells and creaks and ravaged condition of the old house had begun to weigh on me.

And so had Bainbridge.

Angry, not knowing what else to do, I went over to his bureau and began looking through the drawers. They were empty except for pieces of newspaper that dated back to 1948. It was like opening a time capsule, one of the newspaper ads advertising Harry James at Danceland. Sharon and I might well have been there, her in a corsage for our occasional night out, me in my new Wembley tie, eager to foxtrot.

The memories calmed me down.

I went back to the chair. "I want you to tell me about Conroy."

"I don't know about him."

"You're lying."

"You going to hit me again?"

He looked so old and frail, I couldn't even bluff. "No."

He was relieved. "You shouldn't ought to hit somebody like me that way."

"I didn't hit you. I slapped you."

"Still and all."

"Conroy. What the hell's he got to do with all this?"

"I can't tell you. I'm afraid."

"Tomorrow I'm going to have the police come and question you."

He shook his head. "Then I'll be gone." He lifted his Bible. "The Lord will protect me from people like you."

Conroy had scared him, and now I was just wasting my time here. I stood up and said, "If you hear from Conroy, tell him I'm looking for him."

He stared up at me with his birdy eyes. A terrible grin exposed his dentures. "You think he'll care? You really think he's afraid of you?"

He was starting to enjoy himself again. It was time for me to leave. Before I saw Conroy, there were a few other answers I needed.

25

erri Jankov turned out to be in the book. She lived in one of the new apartment complexes out near Mt. Vernon. I'd thought of calling and then decided it would be too easy for her to say no. Turning me down in person might be more difficult for her.

On the way out, I counted three cars that had skidded off the road and ended up in the ditch, and two big city trucks hissing sand from their rear ends. For once the TV weathermen had been correct: A major storm was about to hit Cedar Rapids.

Terri Jankov's parking lot ran to new sports cars, presumably for the single people, and fine expensive new station wagons. I knew just how expensive because on a day when I'd had nothing better to do, I'd spent several hours pricing them.

In the snowy darkness, the lights of the various apartments looked snug and warm. In a window here and there you could see the tiny faces of children staring out at the approaching storm. You could just hear them praying that the weather would get bad enough for school to be canceled.

I was careful going up the steps. I had to be. They hadn't been sanded or shoveled, which was surprising in a place this expensive. You'd think all these yuppies would get collectively pissed off about such terrible service.

You had to be rung past the vestibule, which ended my plans for sneaking up on the poor unsuspecting widow of Karl Jankov.

I rang the bell.

"Yes?"

"Mrs. Jankov, my name is Walsh. I'm working for George Pennyfeather."

"My God."

"Pardon me?"

"I said 'My God.' You've got to be some sort of cop, don't you?"

"Yes."

She laughed a cigarette-and-whiskey laugh obvious even over the small tinny speaker. "I admire your nerve."

"My nerve?"

"You want to come in and ask me questions that may help the man who murdered my husband. Isn't that right?"

"Basically, I suppose."

"Oh, this is delicious. It really is." I hadn't realized till then how drunk she was. "By all means, come up, Mr. Walsh. I'll buzz you in. You come straight up the stairs and take a right. I'm down at the end of the hall, next to the large window."

"Thank you."

"Oh, the pleasure's all mine. The snow had started to make me feel cooped-up and restless. You'll be much more interesting than TV."

When you manage an apartment building yourself, you tend to notice how other such buildings are maintained. This one was enviable. Not only was the blue hallway carpeting fairly new, it was kept up. The faint tangy smell of cleaning solvent rose to my nostrils. The walls had been painted no more than a few months ago, and the trim was without any scarring. I was impressed.

The first thing I noticed about her was her size. She had

to be sixty or seventy pounds overweight, a fact she tried to conceal by wearing a dark silk robe that hung from her shoulders without exactly touching any other part of her body. She wore festive red slippers and festive red nail polish and festive red lipstick, which contrasted with the dyed jet-black color of her hair. Even from here you could smell her perfume, heavy enough to sting the senses momentarily but not in any way unpleasant. But however much the rest of her had deteriorated, the beauty of her face had remained intact, almost eerily so, like a doll's head that had been stuck on the wrong body, a sculpted face with high cheekbones and a gorgeous slash of a nose and a wry erotic mouth with the tiny white teeth of a little girl showing in the flash of her smile.

She put out a hand heavy with rings. If even half of the rings contained real diamonds, I was impressed.

"May I fix you a drink?"

"Coffee would be fine."

Her dark eyes conveyed disappointment. She rattled her highball in my direction. "I hate to drink alcohol alone. It always makes me feel sinful." She showed me her little girl's teeth. "But then feeling sinful isn't the worst feeling in the world, now, is it?"

I followed her inside. It was like stepping into a showroom. A Victorian sofa, with matching period chairs, dominated a living room impeccably appointed with what appeared to be a genuine Persian rug, a large round mahogany coffee table, and lacy curtains that trapped the soft pink light emanating from a small pink lamp in the corner. It was a room meant to impress, and it did.

"Cream?"

"Black is fine."

"Some cake, perhaps?"

"No, thanks."

She laughed. "Looking at me, you'd never think that I liked sweets, now would you?"

She spoke in the tone of all people who hate themselves for their weaknesses.

"I think I'll just stick to coffee, thanks."

Apparently, she didn't like my answer. She stared at me as if appraising a dog she might consider buying, and said, "How old a man are you, Mr. Walsh?"

It was meant to put me in my place, and to establish her superiority. She might be fat but she was not old, her question said. She might be drunk but even sauced she had more bitchy wit than I did. We had one thing in common. She didn't like herself, and I didn't like her, either.

She disappeared then, smiling unpleasantly, as if a small victory in an endless war had just been won, leaving me to park one cheek on the edge of her sofa. I almost felt as if I were violating it in some way. Next to me lay a hard-cover book that had been left open approximately in the middle. A new chapter heading read: "Getting Control of Your Impulses."

I was scanning the first few paragraphs when she returned. She bore the pewter mug on the pewter saucer and sat them down on the coffee table with a model's contrived and precarious grace.

"Do you suppose that will help?"

"Pardon me?" I said.

"I saw you were looking at the book. Do you suppose it will work for me?"

She enjoyed making you despise her. I suppose she hoped that somebody would despise her almost as much as she despised herself.

"I couldn't say."

"You're uncomfortable, aren't you?"

I shrugged.

"You'd rather sit here and pretend that I'm not fat at all, wouldn't you?"

"I really came to talk about your ex-husband."

"Such as?"

"Such as dear sweet Richard Heckart." She smiled again. "Don't you just love men who devote their entire lives to interior decoration?"

"Richard didn't like him?"

"Of course Richard didn't like him. The only two people who had any real power in that company were Paul and Karl."

"How did Karl get so much power?"

"Would you like a cigarette? I've been noticing your pack in your shirt. And maybe you could give me one—I don't inhale them but they do slow down my need for—food."

I got out two cigarettes, giving her one. I almost hated lighting it for her. It was like lighting another man's cigarette.

"Karl was so indispensable that he took over the number two spot, even though it would ordinarily have gone to Richard Heckart?"

"You don't understand, dear. Karl was a kiss-ass. That and his looks were his only talents. Believe me, he certainly wasn't very bright and he certainly wasn't very good in bed. But he had this earnest boyish quality that men seemed to trust and women found very appealing." She smiled. "And he looked wonderful in a three-piece suit."

"So he kissed Paul Heckart's ass?"

"Shamelessly."

"What form did it take?"

"Oh, there was the makeover."

"I don't understand what that means."

"Well, in female terms, it means you take a very drab girl and with makeup and the right clothes, you turn her into a fox. You see?"

"All right."

"And that's one of the things he did for Paul, who was strictly brown shoes when Karl met him. Paul was this sort of chubby, sweaty guy who spent a lot of time serving on church

committees and giving money to his wife's various Junior
League activities. But Karl changed him."

"How?"

"Well, dear, you could start with the hair. Paul always used
to get one of those bowl jobs—literally, it looked as if his
barber had put a bowl on his head and just sheared off the
bottom half."

"That was Karl's idea?"

"That, and the Saville Row suits and the sports car and the
business trips to Los Angeles and New York. Karl introduced
Paul to a variety of things, if you know what I'm trying to say
here."

"Sex?"

She smiled. "Yes, if you can imagine poor Paul actually
getting an erection, I'm sure there was sex."

"How did Paul's marriage fare?"

"Oh, Nedra Heckart loathed Karl. Absolutely loathed
him."

"Did she ever try to get him fired?"

"Many times."

"It apparently didn't work."

"No, but it did succeed in bringing Nedra and sweet brother
Richard together. They'd never been close until they joined
forces against the dreaded Karl."

"So that was the basis of their relationship, Karl and Paul
Heckart's, that he introduced Paul to a different lifestyle."

"That and some kind of power game."

"What kind of power game?"

"I was never sure." She paused. She took a heavy drag off
the cigarette. She inhaled it. "Karl didn't confide in me much
the last few years of our marriage. We were both unfaithful,
it was the seventies and that sort of thing was very much in
vogue at the time, but Karl never learned that it's possible to
give your body without giving your soul. He always convinced

himself that he was in love with these skinny little bitches."
She exhaled now, her wrath formidable. "Anyway, something
was going on between Karl and Richard Heckart."

"Richard? I thought he and Karl didn't get along."

"They didn't. That's what was so surprising. One night,
Richard came over very late. I was up in bed, exhausted from
a trip I'd taken to a fat farm. At first, I thought it was just
some kind of weird, late-night social call. But then I heard
them argue and Richard did something most uncharacteris-
tic."

She wanted to play this out like a Saturday afternoon serial,
with me asking questions, her teasing me. I played my part
and asked, "What did he do?"

She laughed. "He beat the hell out of my husband."

"That night?"

"Yes. There was a great row. Things got thrown around
and smashed. And Karl got a black eye. He was mortified.
He felt it ruined his looks, of course."

"That may shoot your theory."

"What theory?"

"About Richard. The way you portray him."

"Oh, no need to defend Richard. He is what he is."

We were back into her parlor games. There were better
ways to spend an evening than with a fat, bitter woman who
hated herself far more than you could ever hate her, anyway.

"You never found out what the disagreement was about?"

"No. And I really didn't worry about it. I was becoming
very successful in insurance, and it was obvious Karl and I
were through. I'd humiliated myself enough for him. There's
a limit to everything, don't you think, Mr. Walsh?"

"What did Karl do about Richard coming over here?"

"Oh, he told Paul, of course, and Paul and Richard had
this terrible argument. And Richard had even less power af-
terwards."

I could see the alcohol begin to drain her. You reach a point where it really is a depressant, and she'd reached that point now.

I stood up.

"You're hurrying off?"

"I appreciate the time."

She tried to stand up. With her weight and the booze, she was a pathetic sight. I wondered if she knew just how pathetic. No amount of expensive clothes, no amount of clever patter, could disguise it.

"You don't need to get up," I said.

"Are you implying that I can't get up?" she said.

I said good night and let myself out.

26

In the old days, back just before the big war, this part of Third Avenue west was a kind of small melting pot unto itself. You found Italians running fruit stands, Irishmen running taverns, blacks running small auto repairs out of concrete garages that opened onto alleys, and you found the sidewalks alive with children of virtually every color and description. On Friday nights you'd put on a necktie after a long day working at the plant and go see one of the big bands downtown, and you'd find yourself surrounded by people living up somewhat to their ethnic stereotypes, particularly where my people, the Irish, and the bottle were concerned.

Now there was no evidence that any such neighborhood had ever existed. It had been uprooted and knocked down, hauled away and burned out, replanted and paved over. The neighborhood and the people and the colors and the smells and the hopes and the fears of those days when Bing Crosby had been the sentimental and Duke Ellington the dark dream—they might have been a fantasy, and inside my head only. Carlucci, my Brooklyn friend with whom I'd served in the war, said one drunken night, "You know, Walsh, when I die it all goes with me—everything. Did you ever think it didn't exist in the first place? You ever think of stuff like that?"

And he'd been right, I thought, as I wheeled my car into the curb, deep in the heart of a neighborhood that had vanished as utterly as any lost tribe. When you die, everything goes with you because it's all just a part of your mind anyway.

Two three-story office buildings lay behind a shifting sheet of snow, the tops of them lost in shadow and flakes so large they formed a kind of fog. They bore the same address as Conroy's name in the phone book. I'd also written down the home address.

One lone car sat on the wide, empty asphalt lot, a new green Chevrolet even lonelier looking in the light of the mercury vapor.

I tried the front door of one of the buildings and had no luck at all. Behind the pane rose a staircase quickly lost in gloom.

I went around to the back. The wind was powerful enough to nearly knock me over at one point, so that I had to bow my head and walk into the freezing snow at an angle. My footprints on the ground made me think of being lost in the arctic someplace—the only prints that had ever disturbed the snow here.

The back door was identical to the front door, but instead of a staircase seen through the darkness, there were two small elevators, side by side, and ready to go.

I walked back fifty feet to look up at the windows. I had to shade my eyes to see through the shifting white wall.

No lights anywhere in the building.

I wondered where Conroy had gone.

Deciding to check his car, I once again headed across the empty, howling lot. There being no windbreak, I had to do the best I could.

By now, Conroy's Chevrolet was heavily covered with wet

snow. He would have to scrape off his front and back wind-shields before going anywhere.

I leaned over and started the process myself, wiping snow off the passenger window.

It wasn't long before I saw him. He was sitting up very straight, as if he had the key in the ignition and was about to go someplace. At first, I had the odd notion that he might merely have been asleep. Apparently, he'd had a long day and was most likely tired.

But then as my eyes adjusted to the interior of the car, I saw the blood that soaked the side of his head, and saw the splashed particles of brain and bone dripping down the window across from him. It looked as if somebody had vomited up a particularly gruesome meal.

I started to put my hand to the door but then I stopped. This was not something I would want to be involved with anyway, and besides, whoever had killed him had undoubtedly took from his person whatever it was he or she had been looking for.

I put my hand back in my pocket.

I stood for a time letting the wind and snow cut my face. The coldness felt reassuring somehow. Conroy wouldn't be feeling any coldness now. Or ever again. I felt lucky. Whatever else, I was alive.

I began to wonder how long it would be before the police discovered his body here. Moments later, I left.

27

"ou a friend of his?"

"I work for him."

"You do?

"Part time. I'm a former police-man."

"You are?"

"Yep."

"Cedar Rapids?"

"Yep."

For the first time the apartment manager showed some vague belief in my story. A stubby man in a flannel shirt and baggy jeans and new leatherette slippers, he rubbed at a stubbled chin and said, "So he sent you back here to get something?"

"Right." I chuckled. "Except he forgot to give me the key."

"He don't usually forget stuff."

"No?"

"As a matter of fact, Conroy's got one hell of a memory."

Behind him, in a recliner, his wife sprawled in a robe. It was late enough for her to have a face shiny with cream and a head grotesque with curlers. She avoided looking at me, just kept staring straight ahead at the TV where somebody on one of the nighttime soap operas was just learning that he had an illegitimate son somewhere in the jungles of Ecuador.

"Boy, this is a toughie."

"I know it is, Mr. Haversham."

"It's just his temper."

"Tell me about it."

"I let you in there and you aren't who you say you are and—" He gripped the back of his neck and shook his head. "Boy."

" 'Boy,' is right. I wish I could help you."

He looked back at the recliner. "Hon, you been listenin' to this?"

She just waved him away. She was watching TV.

"The missus don't get involved unless she has to."

"I understand."

He stared me up and down again. "Well, you sure look honest enough."

"I appreciate that."

"And you swear to me that you're working with Frank? I mean, I know he hires 'backup' from time to time."

"And this is one of those times."

"Boy."

"I'm really in kind of a hurry and all, Mr. Haversham."

"So he's waiting for you back there at the stakeout?"

"Right."

"Boy." He clapped his hand to the back of his neck again. "Well," he said. He said it expansively, the way people do when they've given into something against their better judgment.

It was the sort of apartment old men go to die in. Everything had the feel of long use, of being passed down from transient to transient, one set of despairs to another.

There was a wicker rocking chair, the seat of which had

long ago come unraveled, and there were faded photographs describing other eras entirely, Conroy in what appeared to be Vietnam, Conroy pointing to a door that had his name on it with "Detective Agency" just beneath, Conroy with a sad-eyed child who had to be his own glimpsed on a terrible Saturday-with-Daddy before the stepfather or new boyfriend came to claim him, Conroy as part of a five-man bowling team high on Schlitz and new silk shirts.

The room smelled of Lysol, cigarette smoke, beer, garbage that needed carrying out, and cold wind coming in through a window that had been smashed.

I went over, past a couch that was still folded out into a bed, and checked the window. It had been cracked so a hand could reach in and open the lock. My feet jangled on shards of glass. The window had been recently cracked, perhaps tonight.

What made me curious was that nothing bad been tossed. The bureau drawers were tidy, the bookcases with paperbacks running to Jackie Collins and Sidney Sheldon untouched, and the one large walk-in closet a model of neatness.

Nobody would have broken in unless they'd been looking for something. The orderliness implied that they'd found it, and without much trouble.

I went into the bathroom, needing to. After I finished, I washed my hands and dried them on a faded yellow towel on the rack. The nub was gone, and so was most of the "Holiday Inn" logo. As I put the towel back, I saw that the door of the long, narrow built-in storage closet was open an inch or so.

The scent of baby powder came to me as I pulled the door slowly open. I sneezed.

The first four shelves contained about what you'd expect. Bic razors new and old, a tube of Vitalis, Old Spice deodorant stick, combs, a Norelco electric shaver that apparently didn't work, an empty red box that had contained Trojans, and several wads of toilet paper that had been used to apply cordovan shoe polish.

I found the dark brown photo album on the bottom shelf.

As soon as I lifted it, I knew immediately what had made the indentation in the bottom of the Vandersee Import-Export crate back at Bainbridge's house.

The photo album was the identical shape and size.

I flipped through the album quickly. All the cellophane windows were empty. You could see, again from impressions left on the sheet, that the book had once held photographic slides.

I knelt down, my old knees cracking as I did so, and began groping around on the bottom shelf, hoping that a slide had fallen out from the book.

Within moments, way in the back, the smell of baby powder even stronger here, my fingers touched the cold plastic edge of a slide.

I was just retrieving it when I heard the apartment door open and Mr. Haversham say, "He told me a bare-faced lie, officers. A bare-faced lie."

A cautious male voice said, "We'd like you to come out here, Mr. Walsh, and spend a little time explaining some things. Do you understand?"

"Oh, yes," I said, pushing myself up from my haunches. "I understand."

28

Twenty minutes later, Detective Gaute and I sat in Conroy's living room, him with a pipe, me with a cigarette. Mr. Haversham appeared every few minutes to glare at me for deceiving him.

Detective Gaute said, "Why are you so interested in Conroy?"

"He was following me."

"When?"

"Today."

"Do you know why he was following you?"

"Not exactly."

"Do you know who he was working for?"

"No."

"Did you confront him about following you?"

"Yes."

"What happened?"

"Nothing much. I used my old service revolver to threaten him."

"I'm glad you told me that."

"Why?"

"Because Conroy told his secretary all about it this afternoon, and tonight she told us."

"I see."

"There could possibly be charges against you."

"I know."

"You might even be a suspect in his murder. Especially since you lied to Haversham to get in here. What were you looking for?"

"If I knew who hired him, I'd probably be able to tell you."

"His secretary didn't know, either. That's the weird thing. She said he'd been in a strange mood for the past week, ever since he started on this thing."

"What's his background?"

"Reasonably straight. Did a lot of defense attorney stuff. Didn't go into the divorce racket so much. Like I say, pretty clean." He said, "So what'd you find up here?"

"Huh?"

"You should see yourself. You look like a little kid who just got caught doing something he wasn't supposed to." Gaute laughed. "Really, Walsh. You should see yourself."

"I didn't find anything."

"Right."

"I didn't."

"We'll have to search you."

"You won't find anything."

Gaute made a face. I wondered if it was over me or if his stomach had suddenly acted up. "Walsh, you used to be a cop. You know what a murder investigation's like. A fellow needs all the help he can get." He turned to nod at a uniformed officer who had just come through the door. Gaute's easygoing manner worked against his blunt boxer's profile. He turned back to me. "I know what you're going through."

"You do?"

"Yeah. You're starting to feel guilty."

"I am?"

"Sure."

"About what?"

"About George Pennyfeather. Those people have got you

"He's the reason I'm fat."

"I see."

"No, I'm afraid you don't, Mr. Walsh."

"I'm trying to understand why George Pennyfeather would have killed him."

"You think I don't remember you, but I do, Mr. Walsh. You were the detective in charge of the case."

"That's right."

"And now you're working for George?"

"Yes."

She laughed. It was a sexual laugh, bawdy in the way fat women are sometimes bawdy. But there was no enjoyment or freedom in it. It was still nasty. That never quite seemed to leave her, that nastiness, no matter what she did.

"Why do you think your husband was murdered?"

"You don't think it was the reason given in court? That little Lisa Pennyfeather was considering having an affair with Karl, and that little George Pennyfeather couldn't handle it?"

"Do you think that was the reason?"

"If that was what was decided in court, then that must be the reason, don't you think, Mr. Walsh?" She spoke in broad ironic tones. She even batted her eyelashes at me.

"Then, I take it, you don't believe that?"

Her mouth drew tight. "With Karl, you could never be sure. Things were almost never what they seemed." Rancor narrowed her eyes; her tiny teeth took on a feral sharpness now.

"Did he ever mention anything that made you suspect any other reason for his death?"

Her bawdy laugh again. "You certainly didn't find out much about Karl, did you? There were dozens of people who would have been happy to kill him. Dozens. Literally. And I'm not just talking about angry husbands. I'm also talking about all the people at the office he'd stepped on. There were a number of them, too."

convinced that you arrested the wrong man twelve years ago."

"Maybe I did."

"So you're being a nice guy and trying to prove that he's innocent."

"Maybe you're right."

"But he's not."

"No?"

"No. He killed Karl Jankov and he killed the Czmek woman, too."

"Why would he kill the Czmek woman?"

"Because she was blackmailing him." ·

"For what? He'd already gone to prison."

"She was blackmailing him for something else."

"Such as?"

"We're not sure yet. But we do know the Pennyfeather family paid her once a month. A check for a thousand dollars."

I tried not to act interested. "Really?"

"Really, Walsh. A check for a thousand dollars a month all the time Pennyfeather was in prison."

"And you can prove it?"

"Without any problem. We've got the bank records."

"So who killed Conroy?"

He shrugged. "We may be looking at two different cases here. It's at least a possibility. A man in Conroy's line of work makes a lot of enemies."

"You really believe that?"

He smiled. "Right now the only thing I believe is that George Pennyfeather killed the Czmek woman and that his family was paying her blackmail money." He leaned back in the chair and said, "They haven't been very good friends of yours, Walsh. They haven't told you the truth. If I was you, I'd be mad."

"I am mad."

"Then I'd quit trying to help them and tell me everything you've found out."

"Right now, that isn't much."

The photographic slide I'd put down my sock had tilted and was now leaning awkwardly against my ankle. I was thinking of telling Gaute about the slide when another uniformed man came through the door and said, "The lab crew's finishing up with Conroy's car."

Gaute got up, drawing his overcoat around him. "I'd better get back there."

Gaute said, "You feel like talking, you know how to get ahold of me."

"I appreciate the way you've handled this."

"You're not off the hook yet."

"I know."

"And I'd really tell the Pennyfeathers where to get off. They've got you running around and they won't even tell you what's going on."

"I plan to talk to them tonight."

On the way down the stairs, I saw Mr. Haversham peeking out his door. When he saw me, he scowled and closed the door.

I stopped at his door and knocked. He opened it too quickly. His wife still sat behind him, staring at the TV.

"What?" he said.

"I'm sorry I lied to you."

"I'll bet you are."

"I am. That's why I'm apologizing."

He whipped his head to the left and said, "Honey, he's apologizing."

She said, not taking her eyes from the screen, "I heard."

Back to me, he said, "She's really disappointed."

"Oh."

"She tries to trust everybody, but it's things like this that really get her down."

She let out a mean little laugh just as one wrestler threw

another to the canvas and proceeded to step on his throat. "I try to shelter her from the world," Mr. Haversham said. "But it doesn't always work."

"I don't imagine it's an easy job," I said, and left.

I drove three blocks very quickly, pulling over to a side street curb beneath a streetlamp that was almost lost in the relentless snow. Down at the far end of the block, I could see another sanding truck headed in my direction. With yellow lights mounted on the top of the cab, it looked like a ferocious metal insect.

I held the slide up to the light and immediately felt sick.

Before I looked at it a second time, I lighted a cigarette and put my head back and closed my eyes. During my years as a county detective, I'd come up against this sort of thing two or three times. In a way, there was nothing worse, not even the butchery some people visit upon one another.

I held the slide up again and took a closer look, and then I opened the glove compartment and tossed it inside. I didn't want to handle it again. Ever.

The sanding truck made a furious grinding noise as it shot splashing yellow light through the falling snow. The two men inside the cab were as bundled up as little kids headed off for school on a cold day. One of them waved to me.

After what I'd just seen, I wasn't too sure I felt like waving back.

29

found a phone booth in the back of a tavern and called Faith. She asked if I could call back in a few minutes—her mother had suddenly gotten extremely upset over Faith's condition and had been calling every ten minutes and Faith wanted, gently, to put a stop to it.

While I waited I got a bottle of Hamms and a glass and sat in the phone booth blowing blue smoke rings at the TV set over the bar where ESPN was running a tribute to Ali. In just a few minutes you got to see him go from a very young man, and maybe the best boxer who ever lived, to this shambling clown in very serious condition during his last fight with Larry Holmes. It was very depressing.

When I phoned Faith again, she said, "You sound down."

"Oh, no. Things are going fine."

"You're helping Pennyfeather?"

"Ummm-hmmm. How're you?"

"I took two tranks and I'm a little spacey. Right now I feel that there's nothing to worry about."

"I'm sure you're right."

"God, I wish I had these tranks all the time. I borrowed them from Marcia." She paused. "Oh, this woman called."

"This woman?"

"Kathy Stacek."

"Really. That's interesting. Did she leave a number?"

"Yes." She gave me the number and I wrote it down.

"You going to bed?"

"Thought I'd watch your favorite show on the couch."

"That's got to be Carson."

"Right. I know how much you hate him."

"He's stayed too long."

"When're you coming home?"

"I've got to drop by the Pennyfeathers', then I'll be along."

"You're lying."

Huh?"

"Things aren't going well at all."

"No. Really."

"God, don't you think I can read you by now? Something's wrong. Your voice always gets tight when something's wrong. So what is it?"

I thought of the slide. "Some real twisted stuff."

"Such as?"

"Child porn."

"Oh, God."

I told her about being at Bainbridge's tonight and then Conroy's murder and then finding the slide in his apartment, the one with the naked six- or seven-year-old girl standing in the clearing of a woods.

"Who does it belong to?"

"Maybe Conroy," I said.

"You think he was into it?"

"I'm not sure."

"How does this involve the Pennyfeathers?"

"I'm not sure it does. Though from what Gaute says, they were definitely paying this Czmek woman a thousand dollars a month."

"And you have no idea what for?"

"No idea at all."

"You should come home."

"Why?"

"You sound real depressed and now I'm getting depressed again."

"I shouldn't have called. I was just being selfish."

"We're supposed to rely on each other, remember?"

"I suppose."

"Just come on home, all right?"

"Soon as I stop at the Pennyfeathers'."

"I'm sorry this is turning out to be such a sewer."

"Yeah, so am I."

It took two beers and three cigarettes before Kathy Stacek's line quit giving me one of those mean-spirited little busy signals.

I said, "Kathy Stacek, please."

"Speaking."

"My name's Walsh. You called this evening?"

"Yes, Mr. Walsh. I just wanted to ask you to leave me alone."

It was the way she said it that struck me as odd. There was no emotion in her voice. "I'm sorry the boys roughed you up this morning, but they were just trying to protect me."

"Protect you from what?"

"From being dragged back into it all over again."

"Into what?"

"The trial. The Pennyfeathers. The attorneys. The police. It wasn't any fun, believe me. When I was on the stand, the defense attorney tried to prove that I was an unfit mother and a hooker and everything. I'm not very well educated and I don't have much money but I do have my pride, Mr. Walsh. I've never forgiven the Pennyfeathers for the way they had me treated."

"I'm afraid that's pretty standard procedure."

"I don't care. It's not standard procedure where I come from."

"All I really wanted to know was if your story was the same?"

"What you're really asking is, was I lying?"

"I suppose so, yes."

"No, I wasn't, Mr. Walsh. I saw what I said I saw. George Pennyfeather coming out of the cabin where they later found the body. I couldn't be sure but it looked as if he had a gun in his hand. At the trial I didn't say he *did* have a gun in his hand. I said I *thought* he might have. If I was a dishonest person, Mr. Walsh, I would have gone ahead and told the judge and jury that I saw the gun for sure."

"You're right. You would have."

"I don't want to go through it all again."

"I don't blame you."

"I still have nightmares about sitting there in the witness box and the things the county attorney said about me."

"I'm sorry again."

"I saw what I saw, Mr. Walsh."

"All right."

She hung up.

30

The Pennyfeather house looked like a melancholy painting, the snow surrounding it blue from the night sky, the yellow glow from its windows soft and sentimental. A wisp of smoke struggled up from the brick chimney, gray against the full circle of silver moon. The people who lived inside should be sipping hot cider and singing Christmas songs in fetchingly off-key voices, hugging one another in vast reassurance that the world was, after all, a good, true, and knowable place, and that nobody was more deserving of this knowledge than they were.

I sat in my car at the curb, the lights out, trying to calm down. They had deceived me—George and Lisa Pennyfeather for sure, but perhaps even David and Carolyn as well.

The snow was crisp beneath my feet, new snow falling softly now to blanket it. As I drew closer to the front window, shivering slightly in the chill, I saw that the festivities I'd imagined were just that—imaginary. They sat in the front room, paying no attention whatsoever to the blazing fire or the soft New Age music that came from the stereo. It could hardly be described as a holiday celebration.

My knock had the resonance of a club falling against the door, something unyielding and final, and the way the voices fell inside, I could tell it struck them the same way, too.

There were quick whispers as to who would answer, and then the scuffle of two feet across thick carpet, and then Carolyn in silhouette stood in the doorway, light from inside flowing around her like golden waves.

"I'm afraid we're busy, Mr. Walsh."

"I'm coming in, Carolyn." I knew how angry I sounded.

"Even if we don't want you to?"

This was the first time they'd pulled class on me and obviously she thought it was going to work, but before she could say anything else I pushed gently past her, and into the warmth of the living room.

David nearly jumped to his feet. "Didn't you hear what Carolyn said?"

I had the impression he was on the verge of punching me.

"Please, Mr. Walsh," Lisa said. "We're spending the night with just our family. And anyway, you've spent a lot of our money and not turned up all that much." You hear this a lot in cases—clients who begin to blame you for their misfortunes.

"Where's George?"

"He's upstairs lying down."

"I want him down here."

"And I want you out of here," David said, coming at me.

I was angry enough that I didn't care, was willing to be beaten for the pleasure of one punch at his arrogant, sullen face.

Carolyn threw her arms around David, breaking his stride, stopping him from coming at me.

"Aren't things crazy enough; do we really need this, too?" Carolyn said. She spoke quietly, but the sadness in her voice was overwhelming. David relented. He called me a few names but he went over and sat on the edge of the couch and scowled in the direction of the fireplace.

"Would you like to come up and have a drink, Mr. Walsh? We have a very nice study upstairs."

George Pennyfeather had come into the room without anybody noticing. In rust-colored cardigan, white shirt, and dark slacks, he stood in the archway as if he were the host at a small, friendly get-together. He looked a little happier now that he was out on bail.

"I imagine you'd like to talk to me," he said. "We really shouldn't bother my family with all this. Not when it's between you and me." He raised a glass of what appeared to be whiskey. "I imagine you're here about the Czmek woman, and Conroy, aren't you?"

My curiosity overcame my anger. I looked around at the family—Lisa and Carolyn spent, David still volatile—and sighed. In my mind it had all been so simple—barge in here, demand the truth, and get it. But if I got the truth at all, the process would be far more circuitous, and it would involve hurting somebody at least emotionally, and perhaps physically.

"Would you like something to drink?"

"A beer would be nice."

"Why don't I get it, Dad?" Carolyn said, and left for the kitchen.

Lisa, nervous, said, "It's cold out, isn't it?"

We were going to stand here and pretend that her husband hadn't only days ago been released from prison, and that two murders hadn't taken place in less than three days.

We were going to talk about the weather.

"Yes, and it seems to be getting colder," I said, doing my part.

"Dave Towne on Channel 9 said the snow is going to continue all night," she said.

"Oh, for Christ's sake, Mother," David said, getting up from the couch, and making another fist of his hand. "You don't need to stand there and be nice to this slimeball. You shouldn't have hired him in the first place."

Lisa Pennyfeather dropped her gaze, looking ashamed at her son's words.

"David just gets excited," George Pennyfeather said. "I'm sure he didn't mean anything by that."

"No," I said, hoping I sounded properly ironic. "In some countries, 'slimeball' is actually a term of endearment."

Nobody laughed.

Carolyn came back with the beer. Raised to be the proper hostess, she had put on the bottom of my glass one of those bright red little tug-on coasters made of cotton with elastic at the top. The beer had a two-inch head, which meant that out in the kitchen half a bottle was going shamefully to waste. But now probably wasn't the time to raise that subject.

"We'll be upstairs," George Pennyfeather said unnecessarily, as if there might have been somewhere else we were going.

I followed him up the winding, carpeted staircase and down a hallway covered with handsomely framed photographs of Carolyn and David at various ages. In one photograph, Paul Heckart stood with his arm around David, who was probably then ten or so.

We went past darkened bedrooms, a bright and enormous blue-tiled bathroom, and finally into a den that was one of those shaggy, book-messy places with soft leather furnishings and throw rugs and a barking walrus of an old TV console. This would be a great place to watch George Raft movies and dream of the old days.

A gooseneck lamp propped on the corner of a small mahogany table provided soft, shadowy light. George pointed to the leather armchair and I sat down. He took the couch.

"The first thing I should tell you is that I didn't know this Conroy fellow, no matter what the police say." He shook his head. "There was a news bulletin on TV."

"You told me you didn't know the Czmek woman, either."

"Well, that one I lied about. I was afraid of getting involved, and going back to prison."

"But of course you're not lying about this one?"

"I don't blame you for being angry."

"Let's concentrate on Stella Czmek."

"All right."

"How did you know her?"

"You won't believe this."

"Just tell me, George."

"I had an affair with her."

We all build up false images of one another. The stupid jock; the happy fat person. Then suddenly we're confronted with a piece of evidence that completely obliterates all our expectations. That was how I felt now, sitting here with a small, gentle man who rarely spoke more than was necessary and who gave the impression of being lost in all respects. I had attributed to him intelligence but not cunning, industriousness but not ambition, and loyalty. If any man was loyal, it would be George Pennyfeather here. If any man was true-blue—

"You did?"

"You're surprised?"

I cleared my throat. "Well—"

"I'm not the type, I know."

"It's not that,—"

"Oh, it is; and that's probably why I did it. I've never been particularly secure about my relationships with women, anyway. You know, here I was pretty old and I'd never kissed anybody but my wife." He shook his head. "I don't know which is more embarrassing now—the fact that I was so stupid or the fact that I very deeply hurt my wife."

"You told her?"

"Yes. I—I wish I could say I did it by way of being honest but what really happened was that I had no choice. Karl had been murdered and Stella—Stella wanted money to be quiet. I had to tell Lisa about her. How she was blackmailing me for having an affair with her." He frowned. "It was a pretty crazy time in my life. I'd also found out some things about Richard Heckart."

I sighed. "What things?"

"I'd been working late one night—this was before the rumor started that Lisa was having an affair—and I saw Richard Heckart leaving the office late. He accidentally slammed a metal case he was carrying against the elevator door and a few things fell out."

"What things?"

"Slides."

"Photographic slides?"

"Yes."

"What did the slides show?"

"Is it really necessary to go into that?"

"Yes."

He put down his drink and stared off into the darkness. "It would have killed Paul, finding out the sort of thing his younger brother was into. They're from a very old family, you know."

"You still haven't told me what the slides showed."

"You're a bright man, Mr. Walsh. I'm sure you've got some idea."

"I need you to tell me exactly what was on the slides."

"Pornography, of course."

"What kind?"

He hesitated. He looked embarrassed. "It makes me feel dirty to say." He paused again. "Children."

"I see."

"I'd never seen anything like it. Small children, boys and girls, five or perhaps six years old. Doing—" He dropped his gaze again. "Nothing ever disgusted me in the way that did.

I—I even thought of confronting Richard—slapping him or something. I felt so bad for those children—"

"So Richard didn't know you knew."

"No; not directly."

"Not directly?"

"I mailed him an anonymous letter just before I went into prison."

"And the letter said what?"

"Oh, about what you'd expect. I'm afraid I was awfully outraged and sanctimonious. The man is obviously mentally ill and probably didn't need to hear—"

"What did the letter say you were going to do?"

"Nothing, really. Just that I was aware of what he was doing and that he should stop or he would be turned over to the police."

"But you had no way of knowing if he stopped or not?"

"No."

I finished my mostly-foam beer and set it down. "Did you ever think that those slides might have had something to do with Karl's death?"

"No; and you'd have to show me very hard evidence to prove they did. I know who murdered Karl. It's just that neither my lawyers nor the investigators they hired were ever able to prove it."

"You think it could have been Terri Jankov?"

"Absolutely. If you'd met her—"

"I did meet her. Unfortunately."

"I can tell that Terri hasn't changed much just by your tone of voice." He leaned forward in the cone of light. He looked very old suddenly. "All those years in prison, I had such fantasies of what I'd do to her when I got out. How I'd make her confess. How my family's name would be cleared."

"Did you see her when you got out?"

"Yes. And—she laughed at me. She called me names and

laughed at me and said that I just hadn't been able to face the truth that Lisa and Karl had been lovers."

"I'm sorry to let you down, George, but I don't think she's the person we're looking for."

He sat back wearily, out of the light.

"How did you meet Stella Czmek?"

"At a party."

"Whose party?"

"One of Paul's, actually. For all I know, they may have been lovers, too." He raised his glass. Ice cubes clinked. "The woman you saw in the gazebo the other night wasn't the Stella Czmek I had an affair with."

"No?"

"No. That Stella was—well, never svelte, but she really took care of herself and she was . . . quite knowledgeable in bed, if that's not too stuffy a way to put it."

"How long did your affair last?"

"Nearly a year."

"It ended before Karl's murder?"

"A few weeks before."

"What ended it?"

He smiled unhappily. "My natural timid soul and my good Wasp guilt. I just couldn't go on telling Lisa that I loved her while all the time—"

"So she began to blackmail you."

"Yes, right after I told her we'd have to split up. One night I'd been drinking and I told her all about the slides and— The day she told me she was going to blackmail me, I saw a whole new person. It's like those science fiction movies where you suddenly see the monster that's beneath the human exterior."

"You didn't have any doubt she was serious?"

"None."

"And so Lisa began paying the money while you were in prison?"

"Correct."

"Do you have any idea why Stella Czmek came over here the other night?"

"None."

"She'd been paid for the month?"

"Yes, but the way she went through money—"

I nodded, pushed myself to my feet. Abruptly, I was tired. I thought of Faith and Hoyt, of the warm bed with them on such a cold night.

"I got the impression you were going to quit helping us, Mr. Walsh."

"I was going to."

"You've changed your mind?"

"Let's just say I've put off making a decision."

He got to his feet and led the way out of the den and down the hall. At the front door, Carolyn said, "David asked me to apologize."

I touched her elbow. "I appreciate the words, but somehow I doubt David said them."

"If he weren't under so much stress, he would have apologized,"Lisa Pennyfeather said. "That's what Carolyn meant to say."

They were a nice family. I just didn't know if there was anything I could do for them.

"Tomorrow may be a bad day," George Pennyfeather said.

In his mild way, he was asking me, and rather desperately it seemed, for help.

"Let's see what I can turn up," I said, and left as quickly as I could.

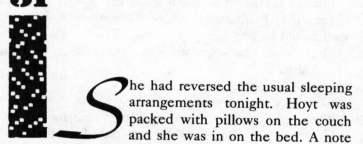

31

She had reversed the usual sleeping arrangements tonight. Hoyt was packed with pillows on the couch and she was in on the bed. A note in pencil and large letters said, "Sleeping pills."

In my underwear, I slid under the covers next to her. She was warm and damp with sweat. Sleeping pills always bring on flu-like symptoms with her, but at least she sleeps.

I smoked three cigarettes. I wondered how I was going to approach Richard Heckart in the morning. I also wondered how I was going to get hold of Stan Papajohn, Stella Czmek's ex-husband, and Marvin Scribbins, the man who'd owned the lot Conroy had listed in his log.

I thought about these things as long and as hard as I could because I knew that the moment I quit playing with them, I'd have to start thinking about the woman next to me, and all that she meant to me, and what lay ahead for her tomorrow.

I tried some more of my failed prayers, not even getting the words right, but trying to address something, anything, that was alive and aware and powerful out there in the cosmic darkness, pleading her case and hoping for the best.

I put out my last cigarette and snuggled up next to her as close as I could, the lines of my body lightly touching the lines of her body, so as not to wake her.

I went to sleep with the fresh smell of her hair filling my senses.

"You want me to go with you?" I asked.

"I'm sure you're busy."

"You know better than that."

"You'd really go?"

"Of course I would."

"That's all I need, then."

"What is?"

"Knowing that you'd really go. Now you don't have to."

"You're not making a lot of sense."

"It's just knowing you love me."

"You knew that already."

"Yes, but now you're willing to demonstrate it. You know?"

"I see, I guess."

"Could we just lie here a minute and not say anything?"

"Sure."

So we did.

Against the curtains pressed gray dawning light. She'd awakened at 5:20 and I'd snapped alert, too, afraid something was wrong.

She'd slept in her bra and panties. She lay still, the smooth jut of her hip against mine. There are times when lust is not only impractical but immoral. Even given what she was facing this morning, I wanted to make love.

I moved away from her, over to the edge of the bed.

"What's wrong?" she asked.

"Nothing."

"Why'd you roll away?"

"I was just getting warm under the covers."

"Oh."

I didn't say anything for a time.

"Were you getting horny?"

"No," I said.

"Really?"

"Really."

"Oh."

I said, "Why did you ask?"

"Oh, no reason especially."

"Oh."

"Well, sort of a reason I guess."

"What was that?"

"Well, because I was getting a little horny myself."

"I see."

"So you weren't horny?"

"No, I was horny but I didn't want to impose."

"I wish you would. Impose, I mean."

"Really? You're sure?"

"I'm not this delicate little flower."

"I just meant—"

"I know. With the mammogram coming up and all. But maybe it'll help calm me down. My heart's racing." She took my hand and put it to her chest. "Feel that?"

"Yeah. It's really racing."

It was sweet, the way we made love. It had never been so gentle there in the warm tangle of sheets and covers.

Afterward, she said, "My mother's going to be over at Mercy."

"Oh."

"I'd invite you, but—"

"I know."

"I wish she liked you better."

"So do I."

"I guess it's because you're about the same age."

"To be fair to your mother, I'm a few years older than she is."

"Yeah, I guess that's true."

"And if I were your mother, I'd have the same reservations about me that she does."

"But she won't even get to know you."

"Maybe someday she will."

"So you understand why I don't want you to go along?"

"Sure."

Just then Hoyt started crying. When he hears us talking, he always wonders why he can't be included.

I went out and got him. His diapers needed changing so I changed them and then I brought him in and laid back down and put him between us.

She picked him up and played airplane, suspending him above her. He put his arms out, the way he usually does, like wings. She jiggled him around and he laughed with his pink little mouth and his merry blue eyes.

When she was finished, she put him down between us. I rolled over on my side and put my finger in his small damp hand. He liked to grip my finger and tug it right and left, the way he will someday when he's a wrestler or a fullback.

"I hope I know."

"What?" I said.

"I hope I know right on the spot this morning."

"What did they tell you?"

"Well, this real nice woman, this Kay Jackson I told you about?"

"Right."

"She said that sometimes the mammogram can pick up on certain characteristics and tell right away if the lump is malignant. It's the waiting and the worrying that's the worst part."

"I said some prayers for you."

"Really?"

"Uh-huh."

"That's really sweet."

"So now you know you'll be all right."

She laughed. "I guess so. I mean, when even a heathen like you starts to pray—" She stopped and leaned over Hoyt and gave me a chaste kiss on the nose. "I shouldn't have called you a heathen."

I said, "Call me anything you want."

When I looked at her then, I could see that her eyes were starting to fill.

She got up quickly and went into the bathroom, closing the door and running the water. She sometimes does this as a way of disguising the fact that she's going to the bathroom. Apparently she's under the impression that I still believe she doesn't have to go to the toilet.

After a few minutes, the shower started running. I wondered if she were crying in there, standing under the blast of the water.

I said another prayer. I still wasn't sure it mattered one way or the other. But I had to do something.

Then I went and got Hoyt's food. It wasn't often he got breakfast in bed.

32

Irma Ozmanski said, "You going over to Big Boy?"

"I hadn't thought of it. Why, would you like something?"

"Well, I don't want you to make a special trip."

"I suppose I could do with a donut."

"You sure?"

"Sure. What would you like, Irma?"

But before she gave her order, she wanted some praise for what she'd done to the office. I didn't blame her. After she'd pushed furniture around, dusted, hung bright new drapes, and lugged out maybe two dozen cardboard boxes with files we neither needed nor wanted, the office looked as good as Don and I always said it should.

She said, "I know I kinda get people down."

"Nonsense, Irma."

"I can be pretty pushy."

"You?"

"No sense you being nice, Walsh. You know what I'm like and I know what I'm like." Her pudgy hand swept the office. "But this is the only home I've got left so— So I just want you to know I'm gonna shape up. You understand?"

"I understand."

"And I hope that someday you even let me help you out

on a case. When you're married to a cop as long as I was, you just naturally pick things up."

"Right."

"So anytime you want me to do anything more than just sort of be a secretary, you let me know, all right?"

"All right."

"I won't put any pressure on you."

"Right."

"It'll be up to you. When I start being your assistant."

"Right."

"Glazed would be great. Two of them."

"Glazed. Got it."

When I walked back through the door ten minutes later, she was holding the telephone receiver and saying, "There's a call for you."

I immediately thought of Faith. "A woman?"

"No. A man."

"Oh."

I handed her the sack. Grease had stained the bottom. I took the receiver, wound the cord around the desk, and sat down.

"Hello?"

"Mr. Walsh, my name is Marvin Scribbins. I'm returning your call from yesterday."

"Oh, yes, thanks for calling back."

"Quite all right. How may I help you?"

"I'm a private investigator."

"Yes, that's what the woman said."

"I'm doing some background work for a client and I wondered if you could help me with a few things."

For the first time he sounded slightly hesitant. It meant nothing. People are automatically hesitant about talking to investigators of any kind. They feel that all questions are trick questions and that they will inevitably give the wrong answer.

"I'll help you if I can."

I asked him if he knew Conroy.

"No, I don't believe so. But that name— Wait a minute. Wasn't he killed last night?"

"Yes."

"Just what kind of investigation is this, Mr. Walsh?"

"It's not directly involved with the murder, Mr. Scribbins."

"You're sure?"

"Yes."

"All right, then. You have another question?"

"You used to own property out on Mount Vernon Road, correct?"

"Right. In fact, I owned two or three different parcels of land out there. Which one did you have in mind?"

"The one where the Drive-Mart is today."

"Oh. Right. What about it?"

"Somebody tried to buy that land?"

"Yes."

"Could you give me the name?"

He hesitated. "I guess there's no reason not to. Jerry Vandersee was his name. Unfortunately for me, the deal fell through. He'd been going to spend a lot of money but then his partner backed out at the last minute."

"His partner?"

"Yes, it was one of those things where two men put up equal amounts of capital. Only his partner lost interest and found some other investment."

"Do you remember this partner's name?"

"I think so. I deal with so many names—"

I waited.

He said, "Heckart."

I tried to conceal my surprise. "H-e-c-k-a-r-t?"

"Correct."

"Do you remember his first name?"

"Oh, let's see; Robert—no; Richard—yes; Richard Heck-art."

Behind him a phone rang.

"You sound like a busy man, Mr. Scribbins."

"You know how it is when you just get back from a business trip."

"I'll let you go."

"I hope I was some help."

"A great deal. Thanks, Mr. Scribbins."

He sounded pleased I wasn't going to ask him any more questions.

I knew it was too early for Faith to be back. But I called my place anyway. It was like making some sort of inexplicable contact with her. There was no answer. I closed my eyes and tried to imagine what she was doing, saying. I felt my control go. On the steering wheel, my fingers trembled.

33

Richard Heckart looked cross as always, like one of those mean, prim male schoolteachers we all remember from our childhood. Not effeminate, just fussy and without any evidence of humor or joy.

When he came out to the reception area, he gave a miserable little shake of his head, as if I'd interrupted him while he was in the process of finding the secret to star travel.

"Yes, Mr. Walsh?"

"I'd like to speak with you, if that's possible."

He indicated the couch across from me. He pulled himself up inside his tan three-piece suit. "I'll sit over there."

"This has to be private, I'm afraid."

He saw how the receptionist was pretending to read her computer screen while actually listening quite openly to our conversation.

He said, "Trish, is the small conference room open?"

"Yes, it is."

"We'll be in there, then." As I stood up, he said, "Would you like some coffee?"

"No, thanks." Given what I was about to say to him, I didn't think it would be right to accept his hospitality.

The small conference room, different from the one we'd been in yesterday, was done in leather and mahogany, like an old-fashioned den. One large window looked down on the rear of Armstrong's department store. Steam whipped out of huge heating ducts. While he waited for Trish to bring him his coffee, I stared down at the people hurrying along the sidewalks. Everybody looked cold as they bent into the wind.

Trish closed the door. I went over and sat down across from Richard Heckart at a small teak conference table.

"What can I do for you today, Mr. Walsh?"

I wasted no time. From inside the pocket of my sportcoat, I took the photographic slide. I set it on the polished surface of the table and pushed it across to him.

"I'm supposed to look at this?"

"Please," I said.

"I take it I'm not going to like what I see?"

From the way his voice had begun to tighten, I knew he had guessed what the slide was.

"Just hold it up and look at it, if you would."

"And what if I wouldn't like to?"

"I guess I can't force you."

"I don't like playing games."

The slide rested maybe three or four inches from his left hand, the one with the fat gold wedding band. He had perfectly manicured nails and perfectly shaped fingers. He would not look at the slide, nor would those perfect fingers touch it.

"You know what's on that slide, don't you?"

"How would I know that?"

"Because you were working with a man named Vandersee and because slides like these were his real business."

"I've never heard of any Vandersee."

"Well, a businessman named Marvin Scribbins is willing to testify that you and Vandersee were business partners who tried to buy a parcel of land from him a few years ago. I'd say that qualifies as knowing Vandersee."

His eyes dropped to the slide. His hand opened and seemed about to reach for it but then closed again and lay still.

"You're afraid to touch it, aren't you?"

He said nothing.

"You know what kind of filth is on there and you're ashamed and I can't say I blame you. That's the lowest kind of exploitation there is."

He said nothing.

"You and Vandersee were selling child pornography— maybe even taking your own photographs—and exporting them, weren't you?"

His jaw muscles had started to clench and unclench. Still, he said nothing.

I reached over and picked up the slide. "Did you ever wonder what happened to this poor little girl, you bastard? What kind of life she had after you and Vandersee were done with her?"

He said, quite simply, "What do you plan to do about all this?"

I don't know what I'd been expecting—some mixture of shock and remorse, I suppose. Certainly nothing as cold as his question.

"Go to the police, of course."

"What if you're wrong?"

"Wrong about what?"

"Wrong about what seems to be going on here."

"You still claim you didn't know Vandersee?"

He paused and glanced down at his perfect fingers. His right hand reached over and touched his wedding ring. He kept his head down. "What if I told you that I did know Vandersee?"

"That would be a good beginning. Then I'd like you to tell me what Vandersee and you had to do with the murder of Karl Jankov and Stella Czmek and a private investigator named Conroy."

He raised his eyes. Our eyes met. He looked grim. "You think I killed them?"

"I think it's a distinct possibility."

"Why would *I* kill them?"

"Because they knew what you and Vandersee were into. Jankov and the Czmek woman could have been blackmailing you."

"That's a pretty fancy theory."

"You may not find it interesting, but I'm sure the police would."

He stared at me and shook his head. There was an air of sorrow about him now, but I sensed that the grief was for himself rather than the little girl in the slide or any of the people who'd been murdered. "I'm not the person you want."

"No? Then who is?"

"I'm not sure."

"I don't believe you."

He stared at the table again. He seemed to be in some kind of reverie.

"Did you and Vandersee take the slides yourselves?"

"No," he said. "Vandersee bought them from overseas. A man in Hong Kong."

"What did he do with them?"

"Sold them. He had a list of men who bought slides like these. They're all over the country. And they're willing to pay whatever the traffic demands."

"The slides came in the import boxes?"

"Right. In false bottoms."

"Customs never caught on?"

"Vandersee never gave them much chance. He only needed one or two shipments a year, which meant that the odds were in his favor."

"He made a lot of money?"

"Hundreds of thousands a year."

"He duplicated the slides?"

"He duplicated them endlessly."

"Where did you fit in?"

"It doesn't matter, now, does it, Mr. Walsh?" His blue eyes had turned almost silver with tears. "There's nothing I can do about what happened."

"Did you kill Jankov?"

"No."

"Did you kill Czmek or Conroy?"

"No."

"Then who did?"

"As I told you, I'm not sure."

"And as I told you, that's the part I don't believe."

He said, "I never thought anybody would find out." He was going into a reverie again. It was ten in the morning in downtown Cedar Rapids and it was eerie.

He reached across the desk and picked up the slide I'd set down. He didn't glance at it. Instead he put it in the palm of his right hand and then closed the right hand with the sudden ferocity of an animal striking its prey. His strength was impressive. He crushed the slide and tossed it, twisted, back on the table.

"Wouldn't it be nice if things were just what they seemed?" he said. "Wouldn't it be nice if I were the pervert everybody has always thought I was?"

I wasn't sure what he was talking about; I just sensed that this was one of the few times he was being honest.

He said, "Things didn't turn out as I'd planned, Mr. Walsh."

"I hope you're going to explain that."

"Not now."

I sighed, slumped back in my chair. "Maybe it would be better for you if you told me everything."

"I can't. Not without—certain preparations."

"Then you're willing to let me go to the police?"

His smile was morbid. "How could I stop you?"

"By telling me everything."

"I—can't do that. Not now, anyway."

"You know who the killer is, don't you?"

"I have a good idea."

"The police are going to assume it's you."

"People have been making assumptions about me all my life. You pay a price for that."

I nodded to the twisted slide. "That's no excuse to get involved in that kind of thing."

"Someday you may know the truth, Mr. Walsh."

I couldn't tell if he was being deliberately misleading or if he was trying to say something through a kind of code.

"Would you give me till four this afternoon before going to the police?"

"Why?"

"By then I'll be able to tell you some things."

"Such as what?"

"Such as who the killer is, perhaps."

"And why they were killed?"

"Yes." He said, "You want to clear George, don't you?"

"If he isn't the killer, I do."

"Then give me till four and I'll have some information for you."

"All right. Are you going to call me at four or should I call you?"

"I'll call you."

"Try my home number first."

"All right."

I said, "I hope you know what you're doing."

The death-mask smile was back. "So do I, Mr. Walsh. So do I."

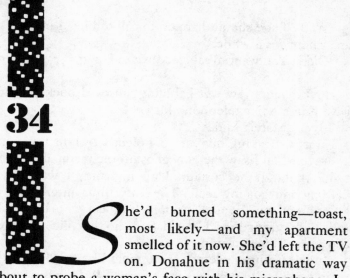

34

She'd burned something—toast, most likely—and my apartment smelled of it now. She'd left the TV on. Donahue in his dramatic way was about to probe a woman's face with his microphone. In the bathroom I found a pink plastic bottle of talc overturned. The damp bathmat was covered with white powder that looked vaguely like heroin. She was scared and so was I.

In the living room I picked up the phone and dialed Faith's apartment across the street.

"Hello.'"

"Marcia?"

"Yes."

"Walsh."

"Oh. Hi."

"How's Hoyt?"

"Kind of grumpy today, actually."

"Give him a kiss for me."

She laughed. "I was thinking of giving him something else."

"I'm sure he's picking up our moods."

"Oh, you mean Faith's test.'"

"Right. You heard anything?"

"Huh-uh. Not a word."

"Well, if she should happen to call tell her I'm back at my apartment for a while."

"Okay. You want to say goodbye to Hoyt? I just picked him up."

Hoyt made a few wet babbling noises. I puckered up and gave him a noisy telephone kiss.

"Bye," Marcia said.

I was just taking my cup of Folger's Instant from the microwave when I saw the gray ghost of the mailman cross right-to-left behind the curtain. Cup in hand, I went into the hallway and got my mail. The only thing interesting was a letter from my friend Salvadore Carlucci who I'd served in Italy with during World War II and who, like me, was a retired cop turned investigator.

Lately, Carlucci's letters were more like small essays as he reminisced about our days in the war. "Remember when you could room and board—and I mean six good meals—for a whole weekend outside Fort Dix . . . for just $10.85? Remember the time we saw Betty Grable perform in New York? Remember the kid from Oklahoma with trench mouth so bad all he could do was cry? Remember how we used to pack dead men on mules and send them down the long, winding mountain roads so the Red Cross people could attend to them?"

As I sat there, my coffee going cold, I began to think back and in doing so realized how many different people I'd been in my life. In the war I'd been forced to be the kind of cold, ruthless man I later learned to despise. Later, as a detective, I'd developed a real sympathy for the plight of most people in trouble—a sympathy based, I suppose, on the belief that each of us at heart is scared and alone.

I was just debating sticking my coffee back into the microwave when the phone rang. Assuming it would be Faith, I jumped for it.

"Mr. Walsh?"

"Yes."

"My name is Stan Papajohn."

"I appreciate the call," I said.

"I'm told you were asking about Stella."

"Yes."

"I guess I'd like to know why."

"I'm an investigator, Mr. Papajohn. I'm working for a client."

"That doesn't tell me much."

"I'm trying to figure out your ex-wife's relationship with her former employer, a Mr. Vandersee."

"Are you trying to be smart?"

"No. Why?"

"If you know anything about Stella then you know just what kind of relationship it was."

"I see."

"They were honeys."

"Do you mind talking about it?"

He hesitated. "I guess not. I suppose this has to do with her murder?"

"Yes."

"Then you must be working for George Pennyfeather."

"You know George?"

"Not really. But he came over here one night."

"He did? When?"

"Back before he killed Jankov."

"Do you know what he wanted?"

He laughed. "Whatever it was, he wanted it pretty bad."

"Oh?"

"That's right. He slapped Stella."

"George Pennyfeather?"

"Yep. Stella said he was a real wimp. But he slapped her anyway."

I didn't tell him about George's relationship with Papajohn's late wife. "Did she know Karl Jankov?"

"The same way she knew Vandersee."

"They were lovers?"

"Yup. Bitch. That was the kind of woman she was."

"Is that why you got a divorce?"

"That and the way the bill collectors were comin' around."

"I thought she was doing very well in those days."

"She was but she got in too deep."

"Do you know exactly how she and Vandersee made their money?"

"Import-Export as far as I knew."

"Nothing else?"

He hesitated again. "To be honest, I always knew there was somethin' else but I never could figure out what it was. I think that's how they made their real money."

"You didn't ever get any real sense of it?"

"Not really."

"Do you know a man named Heckart?"

"Yup. He brought Stella home one night."

"Richard Heckart?"

"No. His name was Paul Heckart."

"What?"

"Yup. I wrote down his license number and checked it the next day. Paul Heckart. Those were the days when I was still tryin' to keep track of who she was seein' on the side. After a while, it got to be too much trouble."

"You're sure it was Paul Heckart?"

"Sure. Who's this Richard Heckart anyway?"

I was about to answer when I heard the key in the door and before I could turn around, she was crossing the threshold.

Given the look on her face, I didn't need to ask how it had gone. She moved quickly through the living room and into the bedroom. She closed the door quietly. Moments later she started crying.

"Mr. Walsh?"

"Yes."

"You all right?"

"I guess so, Mr. Papajohn. Thanks for your time."

"Well, sure. Is that it?"

"For now, anyway. Thanks again."

I hung up. I couldn't ever recall my apartment being this silent. Her tears were a scourge on the air.

I went to the door and knocked with one knuckle.

She just kept on crying. I turned the knob and went in.

35

On the rooms of the dying there is a silence the ocean floor could not equal. In the rooms of the dying there is the first faint roar of the nothingness that awaits us all.

I sat on the chair next to the bed and smoked two cigarettes. I knew better than to say anything.

She lay across the bed, arms out crucifixion-style. She wore a blue two-piece suit wrinkled now from sitting. On the backs of her knees you could see where her hose had chafed. There was a spot of mud on the heel of her right blue pump. On her left pump there was a small tear in the leather.

After a time she quit crying. She drew into herself physically, putting one hand to her nose, the other against the back of her head. She kicked her pumps off. They were loud hitting the floor. She drew her knees up, hose scraping, so that she was in a semi–fetal position. The only sound she made was sniffling.

I got up and lighted another cigarette and went to the window and looked out at the parking lot. I'm not sure I saw anything. I couldn't quite focus.

She said, "I'm sorry."

I turned around and walked to her. "Why would you be sorry?"

"Because I'm not stronger."

I sat down on the bed. The springs squawked. I took her hand.

She said, "I wish you'd quit."

I felt a speech coming on. I put out the cigarette.

"I'm afraid if I start telling you about it, I'll start crying again."

"I like it when you cry."

"You do?"

"Yeah, that way you can't talk."

She smiled and snuffled at the same time. "I do talk too much sometimes, don't I?"

"We all do."

"They did a biopsy."

"Oh."

"The mammogram—well, it was inconclusive, but there are certain characteristics they look for and—well, they found a few of those characteristics. It could be malignant."

"But then again it may not be."

"See, that's why I wish I were stronger. Like my college roommate Sandy."

"She'd handle this pretty well, huh?"

"She wouldn't even worry about it. She'd just go on with her life until they called her. I'll just sit by the phone waiting for the results. I won't be able to think of anything else."

"Then I guess I'll have to break down and take you to a movie. Maybe it's time we take Hoyt."

"Oh, God, you know what babies are like in theaters and churches. I love Hoyt, but I wouldn't want to inflict him on anybody."

"I had a nice time this morning. Making love."

"What if they find something?"

"If you read the brochures carefully, Faith, you know that you've got pretty good odds with breast cancer."

"If they caught it soon enough."

"You don't seem to even consider the alternative."

"What alternative?"

"That the biopsy will show you're fine."

"But I've been through two tests now and neither one of them was fine."

"That isn't exactly true, hon. The first test just showed that you had to have a second test and the second test showed that you needed to have a third test."

"Did you ever have to go through something like this?"

"With my colon."

"Really?"

"Ten years ago. I just went in for one of those tests where they give you a barium enema and something showed up on the screen. I knew something was wrong because they wouldn't let me leave the hospital and they just kept calling me back for more X rays. Everybody in the waiting room knew something was wrong, too. I was embarrassed; I hate being watched by people. But every time I'd be called back, the people waiting would get more and more fascinated with me. They started shaking their heads and looking very grim. One couple even started whispering about me. They seemed sad, as if they were convinced I wasn't going to make it. I was there all morning and then I went home and lay down and I was very scared and I called my doctor. He was busy, his nurse said, and he'd get back to me. I asked her if she'd call Mercy and get the results. She said they usually didn't do that, that the hospital just mailed the X rays over. But she relented finally and agreed to check it out. So I waited and when the phone rang two hours later, I got it on the first ring, and I said, 'Did they find something?' and the doctor said, 'Yes, they found something. We're not sure what it is yet, but there's a shadow on the X ray.' And from there things moved fast. Even though the doctor explained that the shadow might be nothing more than a piece of stool that hadn't gotten washed out by the enema, they sent me to see a surgeon and he took out this piece of white paper and proceeded to draw my colon and show me exactly what he would have to do with it, where he'd be cutting and what he'd be looking for. Maybe I would have felt better if Sharon had been in better health. I was worried about both of us—who'd take care of us if we were both sick? I started to put everything in order. I called my insurance man, and I double-checked on the burial plot that I'd paid for in advance, and I patched things up with my youngest son because we'd had an argument a few months earlier, and then I just waited. My doctor said they'd want to give me the barium test again just as a precaution. So this time I wanted to get cleaned out as well as possible, and I went to the hospital and I was there for two hours and just as I was getting dressed, the radiologist who had taken the X rays came in and said, 'I know what they thought you had,' and he smiled: 'But you don't have it. The X ray is clear.' "

"God, you must have really been happy."

"All I could think of was those old movies where the man in the electric chair gets a last-minute reprieve."

I took her hand and brought it to my cheek and closed my eyes. "It's going to be like that for you. They're not going to find anything."

She lay down on her back and stared at me. "I'm glad nothing was wrong with you."

"Thanks."

"You're the only nice man I've ever had a relationship with."

"Oh, there must have been at least one or two others who were nice."

"Not the way you are."

"Well, that's very flattering."

"You know what I'm afraid of?"

"What?"

"I mean, besides dying?"

"Huh-uh. What?"

"That if they have to remove the breast, things won't be the same between us."

"Oh, God, you've got to know better than that."

"All my life I've managed to get by on my looks. You know that?"

"I know that."

"But if they took my breast—"

"They're not going to take your breast."

"But *if* they did—"

"If they did—"

"Then people would start feeling sorry for me and that would be terrible. It really would."

"They're not going to take your breast."

"You'd start feeling sorry for me."

"No, I wouldn't."

"Yes, you would. At least a little."

"Maybe a smidgen."

"And then our relationship would change. I wouldn't be this appealing young woman to you anymore, I'd be this—thing of pity."

"That's kind of tough to imagine, kiddo. You being a thing of pity, I mean."

"But it could happen. And you know it."

"Everything's going to be fine."

And she started crying again, so hard her entire body shook, and she put her arms out to me the way a child would, and I took her inside my arms and I held her tighter than I ever had, stroking her hair and feeling her soft warm tears on my face, and her trembling body pressed against mine.

Gently, I eased her back down on the bed and got a pillow under her head and took the extra cover from the end of the bed and spread it over her.

"Shouldn't I see Hoyt?" she said.

"Why don't you try to take a nap first? You're exhausted. Then you can see Hoyt."

"He really is your son, you know that now, don't you?"

"Yes; yes, I know that now," I said.

I went out and closed the door. I went into the living room and sat on the edge of the recliner. I smoked a cigarette with almost suicidal need. Her tears were still wet on my face. My hands were shaking.

Next to me, the phone went off like an explosion. I picked it up. A woman's voice said, "You better get down here."

"Where?"

"The office."

"What's wrong, Irma?"

"There's a guy."

"A guy?"

"Yeah, and he's—" I hadn't realized till then how rattled she was.

"There's a guy, Irma, and he's what?"

"He's dying."

"What?"

"He's dying. He opened the door and asked for you and then he fell on the floor."

"Call an ambulance."

"He won't let me."

"How can he stop you?"

"He's got a gun pointed at me. He made me call you. He wants you to come down here right away."

"Did he give you his name?"

"Huh-uh."

"I'll be right there."

I went in to kiss Faith goodbye. She slept. She was as warm as a slumbering child. I tiptoed back out, got my shoes and heavy winter jacket on, and headed downtown.

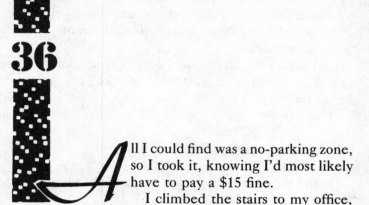

36

All I could find was a no-parking zone, so I took it, knowing I'd most likely have to pay a $15 fine.

I climbed the stairs to my office, not wanting to wait for the elevator. When you do something like that at my age, and while you haven't completely given up smoking, you pay for it.

I arrived at my office door panting and sweating.

I pushed open the door. Irma, her thumb in her mouth, paced back and forth in front of the inner office. Seeing me, she jerked her thumb from her lips, as if I'd caught her doing something disgusting, which perhaps I had.

"Where is he?"

"In there." She indicated the inner office.

"Have you called an ambulance yet?"

"I thought you'd want to talk to him first."

I nodded a thank you and went on inside.

In the drab daylight, the place looked more like a museum than ever. The aged furnishings, the painted steam heat register in the corner, the linoleum floor—it was like stepping inside a time capsule.

He sat in the plump leather chair angled to the side of the coffee table. On his white shirt inside his tan suit you could see a wide patch of blood. He was pale and sweating, and when he spoke, you could almost hear his dry lips crack from fever. "You took a while."

"I got here as soon as I could."

"I didn't mean to scare the old lady."

I smiled. "Takes more than that to scare her."

"I'm not the guy you're looking for."

"Why don't you let me call an ambulance?"

"I want to tell you something first."

"No; first we call an ambulance."

I turned away from him and walked back to the door. In the silence my footsteps made squeaking noises on the old floor. Back when this place was new, men were probably still wearing spats.

He said, "Don't you see the gun I've got in my hand?"

"I see it."

"I told you I didn't want you to call an ambulance for me just yet."

I glanced back at him. "I guess you'll have to shoot me." I opened the door and said to Irma, "Dial 911. Get an ambulance here as fast as you can."

She nodded.

After closing the door, I walked back to the desk and took the chair across from him. He was going quickly. His breathing was coming in small spasms and he didn't have enough strength to hold on to his weapon any more. It dropped from his hand to the floor. I was afraid it might discharge.

"You want to know something funny?"

"What?" I said.

"I'm the straight one. Paul, he—"

Richard Heckart's head twisted to the side abruptly, as if an invisible hand had slapped it. He lay like that a long moment and then angled his face back to me. "I just wanted you to know what really happened."

"You can tell me later. Maybe you'd better rest now."

"I just couldn't let Paul bring down the whole company. Our father's reputation. That's why I got involved with Vandersee and those slides. I wanted to force Vandersee to stop before people found out what he and Paul were doing."

Since he wanted to talk, I thought I might try to take advantage of it. "Who shot you?"

"I'm not sure. I was in my garage—"

"Could it have been Paul?"

"It could have been." He started to say something else and then stopped. His whole body had begun to twitch. During the fifties I'd had a collie who'd died of a lung disease. I'd held him there at the last as my two boys looked on, held him tight so they wouldn't see him tremble and get frightened. Richard Heckart was going into that phase now. "Could you get me a glass of water?"

"You bet."

I went to the door and asked Irma to get a glass of water quick, but when I turned around I said over my shoulder, "Forget it, Irma."

"What?"

"Forget it. I don't think he's going to need it."

Down the street I could hear the whoop and wail of the ambulance. On television, detectives always know when somebody's dead. In life they rarely do. Once, I threw a sheet over the face of a guy struck by a car, sure he was dead. He reached up with a big bear paw of a hand and ripped the sheet from his face, understandably angry with my mistake.

But instinctively I sensed that Richard Heckart had passed on. In the war I'd known a kid from Des Moines who always studied the bodies of people recently killed. While he would never admit it, I always suspected that he sat there and watched the corpses to see if he could find any evidence that souls did indeed migrate. Maybe now, as I stood over Richard Heckart, I was looking for the same thing. Maybe, given

Faith's possible condition, I needed reassurance that we had souls to begin with, and that after our bodies died they did indeed go someplace more peaceful.

"He was a nice-looking man," Irma said, coming up and standing beside me. "I wish he would've let me call an ambulance earlier."

"I'm not sure he wanted to live all that badly."

"How come?"

"Oh, people made a lot of unfair judgments about him—and I think he was also tired of protecting somebody."

"Who?"

"His brother."

"What'd his brother do?"

"Well, for starters, I think he killed Karl Jankov."

"I thought George Pennyfeather—"

That's when the male-and-female ambulance team came trotting through the door, intense and singular in their white uniforms and air of urgency.

They went over to Richard Heckart and started all their procedures.

I leaned in to Irma and said, "I've got some things I've got to do."

"You be back today?"

"Probably not."

"What if somebody calls?"

"Just tell them I'll be back tomorrow."

"You okay?"

I laughed. "Do I look okay?"

She patted me on the shoulder. "Tomorrow I'll go over to Big Boy for the donuts. How's that?"

"Sounds more than fair."

"You going to look up Paul Heckart?"

"I guess that sounds like as good an idea as any."

"You think you're ever going to let me be your assistant?"

"Sure. Someday."

"I'd be a good one."

I then did something I never thought I ever would or even could. I brought my lips to Irma's forehead and kissed her. "I'll talk to you tomorrow," I said, and left.

She looked as surprised as I felt.

37

The receptionist at Paul Heckart's office was sipping coffee and glancing at a *Cosmo* she had skillfully tucked beneath a wide swath of papers. Presumably she hadn't heard about Richard Heckart's death or she wouldn't be her usual indifferent self.

"Good morning," she said, then frowned slightly. "Do you have an appointment?"

"No. But I'd like you to buzz Paul if you would and tell him that I need to see him on a very urgent matter."

"I'm afraid that without an appointment—"

"He'll want to see me. Believe me."

I kept my voice level but I sounded more serious than most people she met at this desk.

She covered up *Cosmo* completely and then picked up the receiver from the small bank of phone buttons. She touched an expert red-tipped finger to a certain button and waited, tapping that same red-tipped finger against the desk. Finally, she said, "Humphf."

"What?"

"He doesn't seem to be in his office. Would you like me to page him?"

"Please."

"All right." She paged. The sound was like that of a hospital, discreet but imposing nonetheless. "Paul Heckart. Please call the receptionist. Paul Heckart. Please call the receptionist." To me, "It should just be a minute. Would you like to sit down?"

"No thanks."

Seeming vaguely insulted, she said, "Would you mind if I got back to my work, then?"

"Not at all."

I wondered if that would be *Cosmo* or the stack of papers. After a minute, I said, "Would you mind paging him again?"

She glanced up. "Sometimes he gets busy and it's hard for him to get to the phone right away. If you'd just be a little patient—"

Just then a pleasant-looking woman in her forties appeared. She wore a gray suit that gave her the formidable look of a country-club matron who had once been a babe.

"Oh, Helen," the receptionist said. "Have you seen Paul in the past twenty minutes or so?"

Helen looked at me and then back at the receptionist. "Yes, I did. About fifteen minutes ago."

"Where was he?"

"In the small conference room in the back, but I think he went down the back stairs. He had a topcoat and valise with him."

"The back stairs lead to the parking garage?" I said.

She did not seem happy with me. There was an order to the universe and I was upsetting it. "Yes, why?"

"Thank you."

I got out of there before they could say anything.

The parking garage was a big gray concrete tomb, cold and shadowy on a day like this one. Car engines sounded like fighter planes echoing off the walls; the air was tart with the smell of exhaust fumes.

The parking place that said Paul Heckart in black-on-white letters was empty.

* * *

At an outdoor phone, I called the Pennyfeathers. Lisa answered.

"Is George there?"

"Not right now. He's gone somewhere for a few hours."

"I'd like to know where."

She started to sound worried. "What's wrong?"

"I'm not sure yet. But I really need to get ahold of George."

"Would you mind telling me why?"

"It would be better right now if I didn't have to explain, Lisa. When I've got more time and more answers, I will. I promise. Now, would you tell me where George went?"

"The cabin."

"Where we were the other day?"

"Yes."

"Why did he go out there?"

"Well, he hadn't planned on it or anything but Paul came over and asked if he'd just ride along. Paul said he needed to check the cabin for a leaky roof. He still uses it from time to time, even though he officially gave it to us a long time ago."

"Thank you."

"You really sound in a hurry."

"I am. A little bit, anyway."

"Well, I hope everything's all right."

"I'm sure it will be."

I left town just as crews began putting up Christmas decorations on Third Avenue. The brightness of the ornaments gave the gray day a lift. Cedar Rapids is very pretty at Christmastime especially, the timbered hills surrounding it snow-topped and serene. The downtown decorations just make it all the more gorgeous.

Unfortunately, right now I didn't have time to think about anything pleasant at all. I wondered if Paul Heckart planned to kill George Pennyfeather the way he had the others.

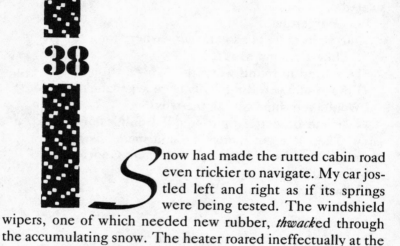

38

Snow had made the rutted cabin road even trickier to navigate. My car jostled left and right as if its springs were being tested. The windshield wipers, one of which needed new rubber, *thwack*ed through the accumulating snow. The heater roared ineffectually at the seventeen-degree temperature. I found it a good idea to keep my black leather gloves on inside.

Finding the shelf I'd used the other day, I pulled the car over and got out. From here I could see down through the heavy forest and the whipping snow to the cabin and the lone blue Buick Regal parked there.

Huddling into my coat, my nose and cheeks already numb with cold, I started angling my way down the road.

In all, it took fifteen minutes to reach the small horseshoe-shaped clearing to the west of the cabin. Kneeling behind the thick trunk of an elm, I tried to see into the side windows ten yards away. But the only sign of life was the fragile curl of gray smoke from the chimney and my own silver breath. A vast silence lay on the cold day.

As I trotted across the clearing to the cabin, my feet crunching through patches of ice on the dead brown grass, I took out my .38 and gripped it tight into the curve of my hand.

I went around back. A screen door opened onto a small

porch where three garbage cans and a tarpaulin-covered lawn-mower stood. My weight on the porch wood was sufficient to make it creak as loud as the cry of a bird. I paused, my whole system charged with anxiety, certain that I'd been heard.

After a long minute, I took another step up onto the porch, leaning across so my hand could grab the doorknob and give it a turn. I wasn't really surprised that it was locked.

Backing off the porch, fixing my .38 tight into my hand again, I started around the side of the cabin, walking on my haunches because the windows were low and otherwise I would be easily spotted. I had gone perhaps ten feet hunched down this way when a voice behind me said, "I have a rifle, Mr. Walsh, and I'm fully prepared to use it. Please set your gun down carefully and turn around."

In one way the words had an almost comic effect. You hear them so often on television and so seldom in life—in my case, never once had I heard them in more than thirty years of law enforcement. But I didn't doubt their seriousness. There was a heat in them, a desperation, and I knew enough to take them seriously.

I squatted and set my gun on a patch of browned clover. Knees cracking, I stood up, turned around, and faced Paul Heckart.

Ever dapper, he wore a gray herringbone suit and a startling white shirt and a red necktie. A black fedora rested at a jaunty angle on his silver head, and a black topcoat complemented perfectly the gray of the suit. In his black-gloved hands he held a Remington, the stock an expensive mahogany, the blue steel oiled expertly. He looked like the world's most fashionable assassin.

He came closer, though not by much. We stood five feet apart. "I wish you hadn't come out here," he said.

"After your brother was killed, there wasn't anyplace else to go."

He couldn't have faked it, that look of surprise and remorse.

He said, shaking for the first time and not from the cold, "Richard is dead?"

"Yes. He died in my office."

His face resembled that of an animal that is just beginning to experience intolerable pain. His features could not settle on an expression but remained fluid in their grief. "Jesus, all he ever tried to do was help."

"You and Vandersee and Stella Czmek were involved in importing child pornography and Richard found out and tried to get you out of it by closing down the whole operation. Right?"

"Yes," he said, but he didn't give the impression he was listening very carefully.

"And you killed Karl Jankov because he learned what you were involved in and started blackmailing you along with Stella Czmek."

"That's where you're wrong," he said. "I didn't kill anybody."

"Well, somebody killed Jankov and Stella Czmek and Conroy and Richard."

"It wasn't me." He was beginning to fold under the pressure. I had the sense that a part of him wanted to hand the Remington over to me and put me in charge. He raised his head. He looked terrible. "I know what you think of me and my—compulsions. The children, and what happened, and all. But I didn't kill anybody. I swear."

"Is George inside?"

"Yes. Why?"

"I want to talk to him about Conroy."

"What about Conroy?"

"Who was he working for?"

"For Richard."

"What?"

"That's how Richard found out that I was involved with— the slides."

"This was when?"

"Years ago."

"And he was still working for Richard when he was killed?"

"Yes."

"Why?"

"Because Richard was afraid that I was still caught up in it all. Conroy would follow me around and—"

"There's something wrong here."

"What are you talking about?"

"All these deaths. There's somebody on a rampage. You just don't kill this many people without—"

The rifle shot was a high, hard sound on the drab, frozen day. At first, I reacted instinctively, not even trying to determine the direction of the shot. I simply dove for the crusted earth, banging my chin on the ground as I did so, stars forming on the sudden temporary darkness inside my eyes. As I struggled to shake my senses clear again, I heard the second shot, this one accompanied almost instantly by a small animal sob, the sound of an entity abruptly dying. There was the unyielding noise of a body hitting the ground, joined again by the gasp and sob of death, and then, as the echo of the gunshot died, there was once more the frozen silence.

The bullet had gone in the back of his head and ruined utterly his swank black fedora, just as it had ruined his forehead where the bullet had exited, leaving only a raw red hole, like something from the inside out, that I did not care to look at for long.

There was nothing to be done for him now. I hurried inside the cabin.

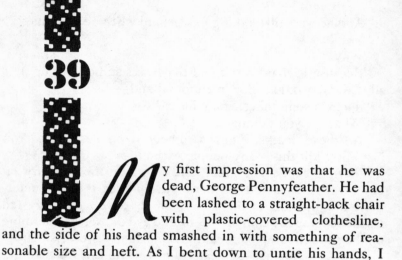

39

My first impression was that he was dead, George Pennyfeather. He had been lashed to a straight-back chair with plastic-covered clothesline, and the side of his head smashed in with something of reasonable size and heft. As I bent down to untie his hands, I saw tossed away by the coffee table a piece of alloy that was probably a decorator paperweight of some kind. One corner of it was a gelatinous red, with hair covering the mucus-like blood.

As the clothesline came off, he groaned a few words that were unintelligible. His eyes rolled white and then closed again.

A small man, he was easy enough to get to the couch, where I helped him lie down. From the sink I grabbed a towel that I soaked in warm water, placing it carefully across his forehead. In one of the kitchen cabinets I found a half-filled fifth of Old Grand-Dad. I poured him a strong shot of it and brought it back to him.

Swallowing, he coughed, and when he coughed you could see the effects of the pain work like lightning across his head. He cursed, which I'd never heard him do before, and he stared at me with what seemed to be a mixture of gratitude and anger.

"Paul's dead," I said. "Somebody shot him."

I'd fixed him so finally in my mind as this weak, soft-spoken little man that his anger was all the more startling. "I should have known what happened and shot him myself a long time ago," he said. His fury gave him momentary strength.

"I don't know what you're talking about."

He tried to sit up. The pain from his head wound paralyzed him at midpoint, just after he'd tried to put his feet down on the floor. "Sonofabitch," he said.

"Just sit back. I'll get you some more whiskey."

He watched me for a long moment, as if trying to literally read my mind, and then he said, in the soft, almost plaintive voice I usually associated with him, "Maybe he'll come back and kill me, too. I deserve it."

"Who'll come back and kill you?"

"My son, David."

"David killed Paul?"

"Yes."

"But why?"

"Because they all knew what had happened and nobody did anything about."

"The child pornography, you mean?"

"That and what Paul had done to him."

"I still don't understand."

He waved his empty glass at me. I stepped over to the cupboard and got him more whiskey. Some of it spilled on my hand. The tart, inviting smell made me want some. I knew I'd better put it off till later.

After taking a long drink, he said, "Do you remember Lisa and me telling you that Paul—our good family friend—used to take David on fishing trips up here?"

"Yes."

He didn't get to the real subject, at first. He was more interested in punishing himself. "You know, I should never have had a son. I had nothing to teach a son. I was just this mousy little man who was fortunate enough to inherit a small amount of money and to marry into an even larger amount of money." He stared over at the fireplace. It was dead inside and smelled of ashes. "He told me what happened. That's why he insisted I drive out here with him. So he could tell me everything. I went berserk and he tied me up."

"You're talking about Paul?"

"Yes. He came over to the house this morning. He looked almost crazy. I guess all these years finally wore him down."

"Why did he want to come out here?"

"Because this is where it happened, I suppose."

"Where what happened?"

His jaw set. His fingers tightened on the glass until his knuckles were white. "Where he molested David when David was ten years old. Paul said he couldn't take the guilt any longer. And he said he knows who the killer is. He feels responsible for that, too."

He started crying. They were quiet tears, nothing dramatic, but you could tell the toll they took by the way the glass dropped from his hand, as if he had no more strength to hold it. "I didn't know till this morning," he said. "I didn't know."

I went over and poured a drink for myself in a coffee cup. It tasted much better than I'd wanted it to. I had a second.

Pennyfeather held the towel to his wound. His eyes were closed. He didn't open them when he spoke. "Looking back now, I can see all the hints David tried to give me over the years. How angry he'd get about Paul for no reason. How he'd tell me that he hated Paul and wished I'd get another job. And so he paid us back, starting with Jankov."

"Why Jankov?"

"Because when Jankov found out what Paul had done, he started blackmailing Paul. David decided to kill everybody who knew but who did nothing about it. There's this great— rage—over what happened to him."

"He let you go to prison."

He opened his eyes. "He was punishing me. And I deserved it. He'd reached out to me for help and I hadn't been bright enough to read the signs."

"So everybody who died knew what Paul had done to David?"

"Yes. We were all—in one way or another, we were all accomplices. Jankov and Stella Czmek tried to cash in on what had happened to David—and Paul and Richard had tried to cover it up." He drank some more whiskey. "He's never gotten over it. I know that now. It—changed him forever. He was always so worried about being manly and now I know why." He gazed off in the direction where Paul Heckart lay in the snow. "I only wish I'd had the chance to kill Paul myself. I would have done it." He looked back at me. "I really would have. If I'd known."

"I believe you."

"Now we'd better find David."

I took the last of my whiskey so reverently you would have thought it was altar wine. "I'm going alone."

"He's my son."

"He's apt to be calmer if I'm alone."

"I don't want him to die."

"I don't either."

"You think you can convince him to give himself up?"

"I can try."

He started crying again, those soft tears of failure and regret that burn like acid inside the mind forever.

I buttoned my coat, tugged on my gloves, put my .38 in my right hand, and set off.

40

The first shot tore a piece of elm bark off two feet to my right and came less than a minute after I left the cabin. Falling to my left, behind a chunk of granite boulder, I saw David up near the timberline. Even from here, he gave the impression of being frantic. He turned, stumbled, and continued his way up into the hills.

I gave him half a minute and then I went after him, weaving my way at an angle up the slope, keeping low and always looking for a glimpse of his blue sleeveless down jacket.

Within five minutes, the cold started to get bad again. I could feel my sinuses begin to plug up and my eyes to tear. By now, I stalked him along the crest of a cove, the river far below gray and cold. I had no idea where he was going and I doubt he did, either.

Spotting him, I dropped to my knee, slammed my hands into the cup-and-saucer for firing, and was seconds away from a warning shot when a deer appeared along the trail above me, blocking my shot. Any other time, the tawny-colored creature, beautiful even on this drab, overcast day, would have been worth approaching just to pet. Today she was an annoyance. I threw a rock to scatter her and then started weaving upslope again, thinking I was closing in on him now.

At the top of the hill, he let go three shots that put me flat on the ground, behind a rusted-out garbage can used by pic-nickers in the summer. There was a pavilion twenty yards away and it was from there, hiding behind tables that had been upended and tied together for the winter months, that he did his firing.

Knowing this was the only chance I'd have, I rolled back down the hill a few feet, got up on my haunches, and started running as hard as I could in that uncomfortable position, angling for the backside of the pavilion.

I was halfway there when I heard the shout. Then there were two shouts, one of them belonging to David. The other I was still not sure of.

Out of breath now, I fell to my knees behind the green chemical toilet the state park folks had planted here in the woods. I had a good view of the tables David hid behind, and an opportunity to wound him if he showed himself at all.

The second shout came again, and when I turned and saw whose voice it was, my stomach tightened and a chill sweat covered my upper body.

Carolyn Pennyfeather, dressed in blue down jacket and Levi's like her brother, came up over the top of the hill, waving and shouting.

"Please, David; please just come back to the cabin and talk to me."

"You know better than that, Carolyn. You know what's going to happen to me."

"Please," she said. "Please, David."

All the time she talked, she moved wide in an easterly course so that she would eventually emerge directly in front of him. Her gloved hands were spread wide, as if she wanted to take him to her, and even from here I could hear the tears in her voice.

The pavilion had a pitched roof and railings painted silver. In the back was a big kitchen. In the summer there would be Japanese lanterns of red and blue and green strung here and caught in the soft breeze, and young couples on fire with love and lust, and grandkids parked on the knees of grandpas and grandmas. There would have been square dancing and beer kegs exploding with foam and the clang of horseshoes in progress. But now, in that terrible death that comes each autumn, there was just the cold and the dead, stripped trees and low, flat coffin-lid of sky.

He fired at her and it startled me. He didn't mean to kill her, of course, but that he fired at all meant that he was much more frightened and unbalanced than I'd imagined.

She just stood there, listening to the crack of rifleshot and the crackle of echo a few moments later. It scared her and you could see on the soft lines of her lovely face the first inkling that this was not the brother David she knew and loved. This was a stranger.

"She's trying to help you, David," I called as I came out from behind the green toilet.

I waited for his shot, and when it came I ducked and dropped to one knee.

She started running toward the pavilion. This time he didn't fire but let her come all the way under the roof, her footsteps slapping hollowly on the concrete floor.

I saw him lean out from behind the tables. She grabbed him by the head and shoulders and yanked him into her arms. She began sobbing immediately.

She gave me just the moment I needed, and I moved quickly, running hard up to the pavilion, edging closer along David's blind side and getting my .38 directly in line with his head.

I let them hold each other until David, too, started crying, and then I said, "Please give me your rifle, David. Now."

He started to get angry, to whirl away from her and put his weapon on me, but she blocked him, falling toward him so that he could not fire.

"Please, David; please. He's just trying to help."

From there, it was little trouble getting his rifle, turning him toward the river, starting him down the hill. I said nothing, just let Carolyn hold his arm and hug him as they moved downslope between the hardwoods.

"You know what they're going to do to me." David kept saying over and over. "I'll never get out of prison. Never."

"David, just try and calm down. Please."

"You don't understand, Carolyn. None of you ever did. Ever."

When the cabin came into sight, Lisa and George Pennyfeather stood in the front yard, staring upslope at us. Lisa looked as if she wanted to wave, one of those cheery flags of social-greeting poise she was so good at producing, but then her hand faltered when she saw my .38 trained on David's back, and she started crying and put her head on George's shoulder.

The worst part of arresting anybody in a domestic situation is the grief and anger of the other family members. The screams and epithets get shrill, and the threats frightening. Today, I saw something even more terrible, though—family members who blamed not you but themselves.

They fell onto David like supplicants, the three of them, enchaining him inside their arms, all of them crying and saying things that made no sense but yet made perfect sense if you understood the circumstances.

I put the .38 away and leaned against George Pennyfeather's car and smoked a cigarette and rubbed at my nose to get some feeling back into it. I wanted it to be spring and I wanted David Pennyfeather to have the opportunity for a decent life that Paul Heckart had denied him. I wanted the sun to shine and the quack of strutting ducks to be heard on the shoreline and the laughter of swimmers in the blue river to be sprinkled like gold dust on the day. I wanted Faith to be all right.

I was lost to my own thoughts when it happened, and it happened so quickly nobody could do anything about it.

He broke from them with great and overpowering force and ran to the edge of the woods, all the time tugging something from inside his blue down jacket. I saw what was about to happen, but there was no way I could stop it. He raised the gun to his face and set it against his temple. Then, in obscene slow motion, the gun fired. David's head jerked away just as the gun kicked in his hand. The roar was incredible and seemed to echo for many minutes.

David died later that evening, after telling his mother and sister what had gone on. He had killed Jankov because Jankov had one day made a remark about what had taken place between Paul Heckart and David. And David was only too happy to let his father go to prison for the murder. David, in his blind rage, held his father responsible for Paul Heckart's molesting him. Paul had been, after all, his father's friend.

For twelve years David had been in psychotherapy. Curiously, he never told the therapist about Paul Heckart . . . but David did manage to sublimate his anger. Then when his father was freed from prison, David began killing everyone associated with Paul Heckart and the porno ring. He killed Conroy, the private detective, because Conroy was about to go to the press with everything he'd found out. A PI who breaks a porno ring involving prominent citizens will find himself inundated with new clients.

George Pennyfeather sat in his living room listening to all this as if Carolyn were relating it in a language other than English. He didn't seem to quite understand—until, without warning, he began sobbing. They sat on either side of him, his wife and his daughter, taking turns holding him and rocking him gently the way they would an infant.

"Oh, Jesus, Jesus Christ," he said, a small man with a small sorrowful voice.

There didn't seem much else to say.

41

SIX DAYS LATER

aith was in the recovery room for half an hour. Afterward, they brought her down to her room in the elevator. They let me and her parents ride along.

In her room, the nurse fluffed the pillows and began arranging the various vases of flowers Faith had received, and made sure Faith was carefully set into bed. Only occasionally would she speak, and rarely was it more than a moan or some broken meaningless word, the voodoo effects of the anesthesia.

In the window the day was harsh gray, winter.

On either side of her bed stood her parents, her mother holding one of Faith's hands, her father the other. I caught myself thinking how old they looked, and then I remembered that I was older than them.

Not even by noon was she speaking coherently. Her father said, "Would you like to get a cup of coffee?"

It was the first time in four meetings he'd ever said a single word to me. I felt like a seventeen-year-old who'd lucked into something pretty big.

In the cafeteria, her father lit a Camel. When he brought it away from his mouth with a farm-tanned, liver-spotted hand, he said, "I don't know what you got in mind for my daughter."

"Neither do I, to be honest."

"She sure seems to like you."

"I like her." I paused. I tried to say I loved her. I couldn't quite. Not to him.

"She seems to trust you, too. You'd think a girl with her looks would've had better luck with men than she has."

For a time he didn't say anything at all. I watched nurses and interns carry sensible lunches on bright plastic trays to small formica tables.

He said, "That doctor said he thinks they got it all."

"They got it early. That's the important thing."

He said, "You be all right watchin' Hoyt for a few days? Otherwise, we'll be glad to take him."

"I'll be fine."

He had another cigarette and said, "You wanna go back up? I told the missus she could come down and have lunch when we got back."

"Why don't you go on ahead? I need to make a phone call."

I walked him to the elevators and then walked over to the phone booth.

"How's she doing?" I asked George Pennyfeather a few minutes later.

"Better. Not great but better."

"How's her mother doing?"

"Lisa's a very strong person. Look how she held the family together when I was in prison."

Yesterday Carolyn had had what the family doctor called "a breakdown." She had been heavily sedated since David's funeral two days earlier. Even with the drugs, she'd slumped into a deeper depression.

"We should have known," George Pennyfeather said. "We should have guessed. What Paul did to him, I mean."

It was something he would be saying for the rest of his life.

Around five-thirty, just as Dan Rather came on the set mounted high on the wall across from Faith's bed, her parents said they were going downstairs to the cafeteria for dinner. I said fine, I'd stay here. We'd spent the afternoon sitting in chairs around the bed, snapping to attention each time she so much as moved. They were not yet what you'd call friendly, but they were no longer hostile, either.

When they were gone, I stood up and went to her. I picked up her hand. Her eyes didn't open. I held her hand all the time I said my shabby little prayer. It wasn't just for her, my prayer, it was for that more abstract unit called "us," Hoyt and her and me, and what lay ahead.

It was dark then, and you could see the street lights burning faintly in the fog of an early December evening.

I turned back to the bed. Her eyes, open now, stared at the ceiling as if she did not quite comprehend where she was.

I leaned in and kissed her on the forehead.

"Why don't you see if you can get Hoyt on the phone?" she said. "Marcia can hold the receiver to his mouth and he can babble or something."

So I got Hoyt on the phone and he did babble. And at the end, Marcia said, "So how's she doing?"

"She's doing fine," I said, and hung up.

In the darkness, in the silence, the TV set having been turned off, she said, "It's not going to be easy for me. Even if I'm all right physically, psychologically it's going to be tough."

"I know."

"I keep wanting to—touch myself up there—but I—I'm afraid."

"I love you, Faith."

I was afraid I was going to start crying. She must have sensed this because she saved me just then. "How's it going with my parents?"

"Pretty good."

"You look like you're about fifteen when you're around them. Tripping all over yourself."

"I've got evil designs on their innocent young daughter."

She reached out through the rails of her hospital bed and squeezed my hand. "I don't want to start crying and I don't want you to start crying, you understand?"

"I understand perfectly," I said but then of course that's exactly what we did, both of us, started crying.

"I thought you were tougher than that," she said as she pulled me closer for a kiss.

"Oh, no," I said, barely able to speak, "I'm not tougher than that at all."